SOULCATCHER

Also by Charles Johnson

FICTION

Dreamer

Middle Passage

The Sorcerer's Apprentice

Oxherding Tale

Faith and the Good Thing

PHILOSOPHY

Being and Race: Black Writing Since 1970

NONFICTION

King: The Photobiography of Martin Luther King, Jr.,
(co-author, with Bob Adelman)

I Call Mysef an Artist: Writings By and About Charles Johnson,
(edited by Rudolph Byrd)

Africans in America (co-author, with Patricia Smith)

Black Men Speaking (co-author, with John McCluskey, Jr.)

DRAWINGS

Half-Past Nation Time

Black Humor

SOULCATCHER

And Other Stories

Charles Johnson

A HARVEST ORIGINAL
HARCOURT, INC.
San Diego   New York   London

These stories first appeared in *Africans in America* by Charles Johnson,
Patricia Smith, and the WGBH Research Team.

www.harcourt.com

Library of Congress Cataloging-in-Publication Data
Johnson, Charles Richard, 1948–
Soulcatcher and other stories/Charles Johnson—1st ed.
p.   cm.
"A Harvest original."
Contents: The transmission—Confession—
Poetry and politics—A soldier for the crown—Martha's dilemma—The plague—
A report from St. Domingue—The people speak—The soulcatcher—
A lion at Pendleton—The mayor's tale—Murderous thoughts.
ISBN 0-15-601112-3
1. Afro-Americans—Fiction. 2. Historical fiction, American.   I. Title.
PS3560.O3735 S64 2001   00-053950
813'54—dc21

Text set in Cloister Old Style
Designed by Linda Lockowitz

Printed in the United States of America
A Harvest Original
First edition
A C E F D B

Contents

Preface

IN 1969, THE YEAR the first large lecture classes in Black Studies premiered at the Illinois college I attended, African American faculty were so scarce on campus that black graduate students from different fields volunteered to teach these courses, with undergraduates assisting them as leaders for small, weekly discussion groups. I was one of the latter. Reaching back, I recall cutting most of my own classes spring term in order to prepare for my discussion group by reading for eight hours a day John Hope Franklin's massive masterpiece, *From Slavery to Freedom*, and dozens of other texts (by black authors) on sociology, history, and literature. In the late 1960s, these works were no where to be found in the canon or curriculum at integrated colleges, secondary or elementary schools. In the universe of academia, they were "dark matter," invisible to the eye. And, yes, I was sometimes tempted to condemn the white teachers and professors I had had since the 1950s for not placing this history before me, but I realize now that *they* had not been taught this material—they never knew what they didn't know, and thus had nothing to transmit to the children of color who filled their classes when *Brown* v *Board of Education* went into effect after 1954 and who hungered for knowledge about themselves.

What I learned as an autodidact, as an undergraduate teaching himself in those dizzying, early days of Black Studies, was that American history on every level imaginable—political, economic, and cultural—was simply *inconceivable* without the presence of black people on this continent from the time of the seventeenth-century colonies.

So, while I have been a voracious student, and sometimes a teacher, of black American history and literature for over thirty years, I was (and continue to be) astonished by the wealth of research and perception-altering revelations about this country's past contained in the PBS series *Africans in America: America's Journey through Slavery* and its beautiful companion book, which I had the privilege of co-authoring with Patricia Smith and the WGBH Research Team.

However, in late 1996 when producer Orlando Bagwell approached me about writing twelve original short stories to dramatize the companion book's history, I was initially hesitant. Why? At that time, I was a year away from completing my fourth novel, *Dreamer*, a complex, multileveled philosophical fiction about Martin Luther King, Jr.'s, 1966 Chicago campaign (and his fictitious double who appears during a riot). I had already devoted seven years of study to this difficult and endlessly demanding project. The thought of committing my time and energy to yet another book that involved both scholarship and unflagging imagination made me feel weak in my knees. But, happily, Bagwell, a producer I've admired since the early 1980s for his professionalism and outstanding character, persisted. He and his team of filmmakers, who devoted a decade to bringing *Africans in America* to the screen, urged me again by phone, fax, and face-time at a Seattle restaurant to take on this unusual project, since I'd already traversed slavery's history in my third novel *Middle Passage* (a fiction that demanded seventeen years of research on the slave trade and another six on the vast lore of the sea). I fidgeted. I flinched, but at the end of the day how could I say no? I'd come to know American life in the eighteenth and nineteenth centuries while writing my second novel, *Oxherding Tale* (1982), and through numerous historical teleplays for PBS from 1977 through the '80s. Finally, I agreed, though I had absolutely no idea exactly what stories I would write.

Early in 1997 we all met at WGBH—Bagwell, Patricia Smith, Steve Fayer, who wrote the scripts for the television series (and was co-author of *Voices of Freedom*, the companion book for the award-winning PBS series, *Eyes on the Prize*), and those responsible for auctioning the proposed companion book. From the very first we agreed that, unlike some texts spun-off from TV series, this book would best serve readers (and viewers) if it could stand on its own as a unique publishing event. On that cold January day in Boston my only contribution to our discussion was to express my desire to generously deploy a variety of literary forms for the twelve stories. I wanted to create, if possible, a diversity of narrative styles that would make each story aesthetically vivid; I dreamed of dramatizing the history covered by the series, of course, but I also wanted to bring a specific technical challenge to every one of the tales, regardless of their content.

But the long and short of it was that I still had no idea *what* I would write.

For months, as I worked through spring and summer to complete my fourth novel, huge boxes of research compiled by WGBH's Research Team arrived on my doorstep. That fall, when I finished *Dreamer* and finally could pore over these reams of black-bound books and the drafts of Smith's poetically written chapters, story possibilities began to percolate in my imagination. Here, in these boxes crammed with primary and secondary source material, I was introduced to facts and historical figures essential for deepening our understanding of America's past and present; the *frisson* I experienced being no less than the delicious shock of discovery I'd known in the '60s. The research for the PBS series treated major historical moments—the Middle Passage, the Revolutionary War, abolitionism, and the circumstances that led to the Civil War—but in doing so it also unveiled the fascinating and often ambiguous anecdotes, ironies, back-stories, and paradoxes that inevitably arise when human beings for centuries live within an execrable social arrangement they know is unjust and fragile and ultimately doomed. Here, in the historical record, was marvelous grist for the mill of fiction: the slaves who fought in greater numbers for the Crown rather than for the Continental Army, in a desperate gamble for their freedom; the frightening (and wickedly funny) dilemma of Martha Washington after her husband George dies; the plague that descended upon Richard Allen's Philadelphia in 1793; the racist alarm Thomas Jefferson felt over Toussaint L'Ouverture's victory in Haiti. On and on, the material gathered by the research team made history I fancied myself to be familiar with suddenly unfamiliar and, therefore, exciting.

All during the month of January, 1998, I did nothing but write, day and night. I cannot remember anything of that month in my life because I read no newspapers, books, or magazines; I put my everyday existence on hold, apologized to my wife, children, and friends for being physically present but psychically absent (I fear I've lived most of my life this way, what with dovetailing creative projects for the last thirty-five years), and retreated from *this* world to dwell every waking moment for thirty days in the unfolding world of my ancestors. In short, I was in heaven for a whole month.

With that sort of concentration, remarkably like Buddhist *dharana* (focus), the stories flowed from me in a dreamlike rush. Each possessed its own particular form. "The Transmission," which was the first fiction I wrote, employed the most conventional of storytelling strategies: authorial omniscience (third-person-limited) to depict the harrowing journey of the African boy Malawi to the New World. "Confession" shaped itself as a third-person monologue (until the very end, only the slave Tiberius speaks). "Poetry and Politics" is a single scene entirely in dialogue without a line of description, because I heard rather than saw this exchange between Phyllis Wheatley and her mistress. "A Soldier for the Crown" is cast in second person, "Martha's

Dilemma" in traditional first person, and "The Plague" rendered as fictitious diary entries by Rev. Richard Allen. An epistolary approach felt best for "A Report from St. Dominique," and in "The People Speak" I could not resist (being an old journalist) the mock-newspaper article as the story's vehicle. By contrast, "Soulcatcher" uses *full* authorial omniscience as it switches from the viewpoint of a slave hunter to perching on the shoulder of his prey. In "A Lion at Pendleton," mixed prose and verse (George Moses Horton's "The Slave's Complaint") structure the narrative. The dominant feature of "The Mayor's Tale" is, obviously, the "Once upon a time" narrative voice usually heard in folk-and-fairy tales. And the final story, "Murderous Thoughts," is composed of alternating first-person monologues, each with a different voice and diction, delivered to an off-camera reporter.

Rarely is a writer given the opportunity (like an actor) to climb into the skin of both Frederick Douglass and Martha Washington, to descend into the fetid hold of a slave ship and join an eighteenth-century slave revolt, to play Jefferson's consul to Haiti and inhabit the psyche of both a runaway slave and his pursuer. For this great privilege I thank Orlando Bagwell. Much credit, I must add, is also due to my superb editor, Jane Isay, for her wise editorial work once these stories began rolling off her fax machine.

Two years ago it was my hope that this repertoire of formal variations would bring a freshness to the illuminating facts in *Africans in America* which, to my knowledge, is the only history text that features fictions commissioned from a contemporary writer. And it is my hope today that these stories, now published separately as a collection in their own right, will serve as something of a time machine for readers, transporting them back to an African American past that in every way critically informed the on-going adventure of democracy and the creation of the republic in which we presently live.

CHARLES JOHNSON
SEATTLE, AUGUST 2000

SOULCATCHER

The Transmission

THEY WERE DEAD, and this was the boat to the Underworld. In the darkness of its belly, the boy—his name was Malawi—lay pressed against its wet, wooden hull, naked and chained to a corpse that only hours before had been his older brother, Oboto. Down there, the air was curdled, thick with the stench of feces and decaying flesh. Already the ship's rats were nibbling at Oboto's cold, stiff fingers. Malawi screamed them away whenever they came scurrying through a half a foot of salt water toward his brother's body. He held Oboto as the boat thrashed, throwing them from side to side, and the rusty chains bit deeper into his wrists. But by now, after seven weeks at sea, the rats were used to screams, moaning, and cries in the lightless entrails of the ghost ship. All night, after the longhaired, lipless phantoms drove them below—the men into the hold, the females into the longboats and cabins, the children under a tarpaulin on deck—Malawi heard the wailing of the other one hundred captives, some as they clawed at him for more room. (Perhaps, he thought, this was why the phantoms clipped their

1

nails every few days.) He couldn't always understand the words of the others, but Malawi gleaned enough to gather from his yokefellows that they were in the hands of white demons taking them to hell where they would be eaten. Many of the others were from different tribes and they spoke different tongues. Some, he remembered, had been enemies of his people, the Allmuseri. Others traded with the merchants of his village, men like his father Mbwela, who was a proud man, one wealthy enough to afford two wives. But that was before he and Oboto were captured. They were no longer Hausa, Tefik, Fulani, Ibo, Kru, or Fanti. Now they were dead, one and all, and destined for the Underworld.

Every day since this journey began, Malawi had lost something; now he wondered if there was anything left to lose.

They had been herded after their long trek from the lush interior to the bustling trading fort overlooking the sea. They came in chains, shackled in twos at their necks, in a coffle that contained forty prisoners, a flock of sheep, and an ostrich. When they arrived at twilight, their feet were crusted with mud and their backs stung from the sticks their captors—warriors from the nearby Asante tribe—used to force them up whenever they fell during the exhausting monthlong march. It was there, on that march, that the horrors began. Wearily, Malawi walked chained to Oboto. His father, Mbwela, and mother, Gwele (Mbwela's youngest wife), were shackled in front of him. His mother stumbled. One of the Asante struck her, and Gwele fought back, scratching at his eyes until he plunged a knife into her belly. In a rage such as Malawi had never seen, his father fell upon the Asante warrior, beating him to the ground, and would have killed him had not another of their captors swung his sword and unstrung Mbwela's head, but with a cut so poorly delivered his father did not die instantly but instead lay bleeding on the ground as the coffle moved on, with Mbwela cursing their captors, their incompetence, telling them how he would have done the beheading right.

How long it took to reach the fort, Malawi could not say. But he remembered their captors fired rifles to announce the coffle's arrival. Cannons at the fort thundered back a reply. Men fluent in several languages lifted their robes and ran to the fort's entrance to meet them. Their Asante captors chanted, *Hodi, hodi, hodi*, asking permission to trade. The dragomen replied, *Karibu*, meaning they could, and then Malawi and the other prisoners were driven toward the receiving house as people inside the fort pointed and stared. Like slices of walking earth, they must have seemed, so chalky from their long trek, a few stumbling, some bleeding from their feet, mothers long since mad, their eyes streaming and unseeing, carrying dead children, the rest staring round the fort in shock and bewilderment.

And Malawi was one of those. The bustling, slave market was like a dream—or, more exactly, like yet another nightmare from which he could not awaken, no matter how hard he rubbed his eyes. There were harem dancers in brightly colored costumes. Magnificent horses ridden by vast-bearded Arab traders who exchanged the cracking-fingers greeting of the coast. Bazaars. And musicians picking up the air and playing it on their *koras,* as if everyone had come from all over the earth to an unholy festival. In this place human life was currency, like a cowrie shell. Starving families brought their children to sell. Slaves, stripped naked, were held down by other black men as the strangely dressed phantoms branded their shoulders with red-hot pieces of bent wire. They'd been shaved clean, soaked in palm oil. And when the wire touched their skin, burning flesh blended with rich food smells in the market and made Malawi cough until his eyes watered. Then, when his vision cleared, he saw along the beach, just below the warehouses, phantoms bartering for black flesh. They traded firelocks, liquor, glittering beads, and textiles for people from the Angola, Fula, Sesi, and Yoruba tribes. If they resisted or fought back, they were whipped until blood cascaded from their wounds. The phantoms forced open their mouths to examine their teeth and gums as if they were livestock and, laughing, fingered their genitals. They paid one hundred bars apiece for each man; seventy-five bars for each woman. Malawi, whose father had been a merchant, saw that what they called a "bar" was worth a pound of black gunpowder or a fathom of cloth, and he saw that they accepted no children under the height of four feet four inches.

What, Malawi wondered, had he and the others done to deserve this? And, instantly, he knew: Those being sold were debtors. They were thieves. They were tribesmen who refused to convert to Islam. Were guilty of witchcraft. Or refused to honor the ruling tribe in their region. Or they'd been taken prisoner during tribal wars, just as he and Oboto had been captured.

He saw a bare-chested ghost, one with a goatish laugh and reddish whiskers, arguing with an Asante trader chewing on a khat leaf, yelling that the wrinkled old man he'd brought to sell, who was sweating and looked ill, had been drugged to conceal his sickness. No, *that* one the ghost didn't want. Not the elderly. Only the healthy men who could work, the young women who could bear, and the children. He and his brother would surely be picked—Malawi was sure of that—or at least they would choose Oboto, who was strong, with tightly strung muscles and sharp features like the tribes of the far north. Yes, they would want a man as strikingly beautiful, as brave and wise, as his brother.

Oboto touched Malawi's arm just before they were pushed into the warehouse, and Malawi saw—away in the distance beneath a day-old moon—a vessel a hundred times the size of the thatch-roofed homes in his village, with sails like white bird wings and great, skeletal trees springing from its deck and piercing the clouds. This he heard the phantoms call the *Providence*. Then it was dark as they were shoved into the warehouses. Families in his coffle were separated—husbands from wives; children from their parents—so those in their cells, then later on the ship, could not *talk* to each other. By some miracle, one he thanked his ancestors for, they'd blundered and not separated him from his brother, who had seen twenty harvests, five more than Malawi himself.

That night their jailers fed them a porridge made from

roots and grainy honey beer. As they ate, Oboto told him, "Don't be afraid, little brother."

Malawi was indeed afraid but did not want to anger Oboto. "I'm not, as long as you are here—"

"No"—his brother cut him off—"*listen* to me. Even if I am *not* here, you must not be afraid. Malawi, I have been watching these people who raided our village, and the ones from the ship...They are not strong."

"But they have many guns," said Malawi, "and chains and great ships!"

"And they bleed when they are cut." Oboto moved closer to him as a guard passed their cell. He whispered, "I've seen them faint in the sun, and I watched one from that ship cry when he passed water, as if he was afflicted and doing so was painful. Did you see some of them up close? Their rotten teeth, I mean. A few are missing fingers. Or a hand. They touch others in places forbidden, and all the while they look afraid, fingering their rifles, looking over their shoulders. Their mothers have not yet finished with them. They are barbarians. Malawi, I *don't* think the spirits respect them. How could they? They smell bad. They are unclean. They are dead *here*"—he touched his chest above his heart—"not us. Some of the white men I saw, the ones with the whips, grovel before others in fear and have stripes on their backs as if they were slaves. The ones doing the hardest work, unloading crates from the ship for trade, don't understand as many tongues as you or I."

"Yes..." Malawi nodded slowly, for his brother spoke well, as always. "I saw that." As a merchant's son, he'd picked up enough Ibo and Bantu to converse passably well when he accompanied Mbwela on trips to buy and sell goods. And he'd seen one of the phantoms, a young man close to his brother's age, fall down in the heat when unloading a crate of goods from the *Providence*, and because he was slow in rising, one of the other ghosts beat him, bloodying his mouth. He'd seemed different from the other devils. His nose was hooked like that of a hornbill beneath blue eyes that could have been splinters from the sky. This was probably his first trip to Africa and it seemed no one had told him that it was a good idea to take fluids all day, even a little, because your body was constantly losing moisture, whether you were perspiring or not. "But," said Malawi, "I *am* afraid of them. I'm sorry…"

"Don't be sorry." Oboto touched Malawi's arm gently. "I was afraid too when I saw them burning the village. When our parents died. And I prayed to our ancestors to let me die—yes, I did that during the journey here—but they helped me understand."

"What?" said Malawi. "Why they have taken so much from us?"

"No, they showed me what they cannot take. And I will show you."

Malawi knew—as their captors could not—that before the raid on their village Oboto was destined to be a *griot*, a living book who carried within himself, like a treasure, his people's entire history from time immemorial. Its recitation took three full days. When he was a child all the adults agreed that Oboto's gift of recall distinguished him for this duty, and from his fifth harvest he could be seen trailing behind gruff, old Ndembe, who was *griot* then but getting a bit forgetful in his sixties, repeating after his teacher every chapter of their tribe's history. He learned their songs for war and weddings, the words they sang when someone died or was born. He learned the chronicle of their kings and commoners, the exploits of their heroes, folklore, and words for every beast, plant, and bird as well as the rhymes their women sang when they made *fufu*, taking into himself one piece of their culture at a time, then stitching it into an ever-expanding tapestry that covered centuries of his people's hopes and dreams, tragedies and victories. Now Malawi realized their village had not been wiped from the face of the world; its remains were kept inside Oboto. And during that night in the warehouse, while the other prisoners wailed or wept, Oboto began to teach his younger brother, transmitting all he knew, beginning with the story of how their gods created the world, and then the first man and woman.

Oboto continued after he and Malawi were bathed, branded, and brought on board the *Providence*. During the night they were kept below, tightly packed together, and forced to lie on their right sides to lessen the pressure on their hearts. Those on the ship's right side faced forward; those on the left faced the stern. Hatches and bulkheads had been grated and apertures cut around the deck to improve the circulation of air, though in those depths Malawi wheezed when he whispered back the ancient words his brother chanted.

Come morning, they were forced topside. The phantoms

covered their mouths with rags, went into the hold to drag from below those prisoners who'd died during the night, and then by 9 A.M. cleaned this unholy space with chloride lime so it could be inspected by the ship's captain. Up above, more phantoms washed and scrubbed the decks and splashed buckets of salt water on Malawi and the others, then from buckets fed them a pasty gruel the color of river mud in messes of ten. And all the while, Oboto quietly sang to his brother—in a language their captors could not under-stand—how their people long ago had navigated these very waters to what the phantoms called the New World, leaving their hieroglyphics and a calendar among the Olmecs, and a thousand years earlier ventured east, sprinkling their seed among the Dravidians before their cities were destroyed by Aryans who brought the Vedas and caste system to enslave them. On and on, like a tapestry, Oboto unfurled their past, rituals, and laws in songs and riddles as they ate or when the phantoms shaved their hair and clipped their nails every few days.

Slowly, after weeks of suffering, it dawned on Malawi that this transmission from his brother, upon which he fas-tened his mind night and day like a prayer, was holding madness at bay. It left him no time to dwell on his despair. Each day the prisoners were brought together for exercise. To dance and sing African melodies beneath mist-blurred masts and rigging that favored the webwork of a spider. Week after week, Oboto used that precious time to teach, at pains to pass along as much of their people's experiences as his younger brother could absorb, though after six weeks

Malawi saw he was weakening. His voice grew fainter, so frail that at night when they lay crushed together, Malawi had to place his ear close to Oboto's lips, catching the whispered words as his brother's chest rose and fell, each of his weak exhalations a gift from a world they would never see again.

When Oboto's wind was gone, Malawi held him close and chanted his brother's spirit safely on its journey to join their ancestors and he kept the rats away. The hatch creaked open. Sunlight spilled into the hold, stinging his eyes. The phantoms came below cursing—they were always cursing—and drove the prisoners onto the deck. One of them, the hook-nosed phantom, began unchaining Malawi from Oboto. "I guess he was some kind of kin to you, wasn't he? That's too bad. I've lost family too, so I guess I know how you feel." He removed the last of the shackles from Oboto, then stood back, waiting for Malawi to release his brother. "Go on now, you can turn him loose. He's dead."

Malawi did not let go. He tried to lift his brother, slipping his arms under Oboto's shoulders, but found him too heavy. The phantom watched him struggle for a moment, then took Oboto by his feet, and together they carried the body onto the deck, with Malawi still singing his people's funeral songs. They stepped to the rail, Malawi blinking back tears by then, the edges of his eyes feeling blurred. Then he and the phantom swung his brother overboard, dropping him into wind-churned waters. Instantly, Oboto disappeared beneath the roily waves. For a few seconds Malawi's heart felt so still he wondered if he might be dead, too, then involuntarily the words he'd learned came flooding back into his thoughts, and he knew there was much in him—beyond the reach of the ghosts—that was alive forever.

The phantom, his yellow hair flattened to his forehead by spray, was watching Malawi closely, listening to the lay on his lips. He was very quiet. Malawi stopped. The boy said, "Naw, go on. I don't understand what you're singing, but I like it. It's beautiful. I want to hear more...C'mon."

Malawi looked at him for a moment, unable to understand all his strange words. He glanced back down at the waters, thinking that Oboto's songs had only taken him so far. Just to before the time his village was raided. His people's chronicle was unfinished. New songs were needed. And these *he* must do. Hesitantly at first, and then with a little more confidence, he began weaving the events since his and Oboto's capture onto the last threads his brother had given him.

Malawi sang and the phantom listened.

Confession

"Y'ALL WANT ME to sit there?" he said, nodding toward the barrel amiddlemost the old barn because his hands were tied behind his back. Tiberius was wearing a linen frock and red velvet waistcoat. He was thin, clubfooted, and not too happy that the militiamen had brought him back to Colonel Hext's place after what he and the others had done to the old man's wife. But they hadn't killed him, as they'd done with fourteen of his co-conspirators—laying waste to them in a one-sided battle—and maybe, Tiberius thought, they'd let him live if he just did what they asked. He sat down heavily on the barrel, taking just a moment to glance round at the bins of grain, the lofts of hay and straw overhead, and the frail light shafting down from cracks in the roof to the spot where they'd placed him. "All right now, I'm sittin' down, just like you asked, but you don't have to *push*. What's that? You want to know *why* I joined up with Jemmy?"

Tiberius looked down at his bare feet, took a long breath, then his eyes fluttered up at the three white men surrounding him. They were passing a flask of home brew between them. Of the trio he recognized two. Mr. Hutchenson, owner of the general store in Stono. Tiberius placed his age at forty. Forty-five. He wore a pair of riding boots and a tattered balandranas. His eyes were a bit red-webbed from the whiskey, his chestnut hair was thinning, and Hutchenson looked at him with a profound sadness, or so Tiberius thought. He'd ran errands for his Bathurst family since he was a boy, and prayed that Hutchenson, if no one else, would understand how his life had been turned upside down in the last twenty-four hours—or, more precisely, since the king of Spain promised to shelter and protect runaway Negroes if they made it to Augustine. The other man he knew was Ethan Whittaker, an overseer with a gray Cathedral beard, who worked on the farm of Tiberius's master, William Boswell, and Tiberius was more than a little afraid of him, seeing how ruthlessly the heavyset Whittaker drove blacks at planting time; he was drumming a short-handled whip over and over against his palm. The last man—Ethan called him Colonel Bull—was dressed in a travel-stained coat and had a double-barreled gun loaded with buckshot hitched under his arm. He had the air of a parson or maybe a politician, somebody important at least, but Tiberius'd never seen him before—or had he?—so when he spoke, staring up at the three men standing over him, he directed his words at Hutchenson.

"Sir, you *know* me. I ain't never been one for trouble, or for fightin', or steppin' out of line in any way. Ain't that so? I was born right here, not like Jemmy and them others who come from Africa. I played with your children when we was growin' up. You remember that? I don't know nothin' *but* here. And I always been thankful Mastah Boswell let me work in the house, seeing how I can't get around too well. You ask him, he'll tell you what a good worker I am. I'm always hup before *any*body at the house, even before the daylight horn is blown to wake hup the field hands. It takes me time to walk from the quarters, but I'm there before Mastah Boswell, wearin' his Beard box, gets outta that big bed with its pewterized nickel headboard. See, I'm the one lays out every day his razors imported from England—he likes a different one every morning, you know? I lays out his linen shirt with lawn ruffles on the sleeves, his cravat, and breeches. If it's cold, I'm the one lights the fireplace downstairs, and I carries coal in a pan to all the other fireplaces upstairs and down—it stays colder in them second-floor rooms than downstairs, you know. And it's me makes sure Mastah Boswell's breakfast is just like he wants it. Toast with a li'l flavor of woodsmoke in it. And he likes his coffee roasted and ground no more'n two hours before I serves it to him. His wife, well, she favors egg bread, grilled fowl, bricks of cheese, and fish from New Orleans, along with ice water and mint tea in the morning. You ask them if I don't make that old cook Emma have everything just so on the table, with the pewter bowls and plates set out right pretty, before the mastah and missus come downstairs."

He saw Hutchenson nodding. He'd eaten more than once at Boswell's home, knew how much effort went into preparing those elaborate meals, and Tiberius felt consoled by the slight upturn at the corner of his lips. "I've always done my best by 'em, and read my Bible like they wanted. You know, just between you'n me, some folks in the quarters didn't like me much 'cause I worked in the house. I *told* 'em it was on account of my affliction that Mastah Boswell didn't send me to the fields. But that didn't change their minds. They still thought I had it easier than they did. I swear, sometimes I felt like I was livin' in two worlds, just 'cause I worked in the house. On Sunday, the day y'all give us to ourselves, I'd bring food the mastah and missus didn't eat over to that spot near the general store where coloreds get together to talk and dance and such. If Mastah Boswell complained to his wife 'bout one of the field hands, I'd take that fellah aside and tell him what I heard so Mistah Whittaker there wouldn't wind up havin' to whip him. What's that? How'd I meet Jemmy? Yessir, all right. I'll talk about that. Just let me collect my thoughts a li'l…"

The white men waited. Tiberius, facing the open barn door, could see other Carolina militiamen bringing their bound captives to Hext's farm. The sky above Colleton County was fast losing light. He found it hard to swallow, but cleared his throat, licked his dry lips, and went on:

"I reckon Jemmy come to St. Paul's Parish 'bout a year ago, him and a wagonload of other saltwater Negroes. That's what we call them come straight from Africa. I don't know who his mastah is. At first I didn't pay them no mind when I seen them on Sundays at the gatherin' place. I couldn't *talk* to most of them, they bein' from Angola and all. They couldn't read or figure. Jemmy, he spoke better English than them others. I guess what they talked was Portuguese. It sounds a li'l bit like Spanish, don't it? Thing is, there was somethin' 'bout Jemmy that was...different. Oh no, I'm not just talkin' 'bout the way Jemmy looked. They was all big, strappin' boys. Jemmy stood six feet five. You got to figure they *had* to be strong 'cause workin' rice broke so many people down. Visit any of the quarters, and you'll find somebody got malaria. Cholera. Whooping cough. The children *keep* intestinal worms. So, yessir, Jemmy, he was fit. But more'n that, he had somethin'...*inside*. You could see it in his eyes. The way he looked right through you. If I recollect rightly, them Angolans was workin' on a road crew round the time we heard about the Spanish king's proclamation. That was *last* Sunday. Della, she took a newspaper from Mastah Boswell's study, and Jemmy asked me to read it, which I did, tellin' 'em 'bout how slaves who fled to the Presidio at St. Augustine, Florida, was free. Jemmy listened real close when I read that newspaper. His eyes got real quiet. Then he told the others what I said in Portuguese. Just 'bout that time, Mistah Whittaker, *you* come out of Mistah Hutchenson's store, seen what we was doin', and ripped that paper right outta my hands. Jemmy snatched it *back*. And him doin' that liked to make you so mad"— Tiberius laughed, then caught himself—"you commenced to beatin' on him with a harness strap. I ain't never seen you so wild. But Jemmy took it straight up without makin' a sound. Didn't take his eyes off you either or move until finally you was all sweaty and breathin' hard and tuckered out, and just threw down that strap and rode off. You remember that last Sunday?"

The other white men looked quizzically at Whittaker, whose cheeks flushed bright red. The muscles around his eyes tightened. He spat a foot from where Tiberius sat, then turned away.

"Yeah," he nodded, "Jemmy had that effect on lots of people. It was like there was somethin' inside him too heavy to move. Excuse me? Come again, Mistah Hutchenson? Was *I* afraid of Jemmy? Well, yessir, I suppose I was. And… What?…If I was scared, why'd I join up with him? Oh sure, I was just getting to that…" Tiberius leaned forward, stretching out his arms behind him to take the pressure of the ropes off his wrists, then sat back, both feet planted on either side of the crate. "The way it come 'bout was when I went to the meetin' place this mornin'. When I got there I was surprised. Wasn't nobody playin' music. Or dancin'. Or carousin'. They was all sittin' together under a tree, and Jemmy was right in the middle. I smelled liquor. I turned round to leave, but Jemmy told me to sit down. They was all starin' at me. 'Bout eighteen field hands. Fellahs you didn't fool with. I'm talkin' 'bout men so tired from that awful work in the rice fields that in the morning some of 'em was so stiff and sore they couldn't bend over to put on their shoes. Men that'd cut you just as soon as look at you. And at one time or another, Jemmy'd either gone heads up with every one of 'em, or backed 'em down, or done somethin' to make them respect him. I figured, yeah, maybe I better sit down. Once I found a place, Jemmy went back to talkin'. He talked a *long* time. Listenin' to him, I felt maybe like I was in church or somethin'. He was citin' all the things—

horrible things—white people had done. Like cripplin' runaways. Castratin' 'em. Pesterin' the women. Workin' the field
hands 'til they dropped in the water, and all that evil, says
Jemmy, was done just so people like Mastah Boswell could
have his fresh coffee and grilled fowl every morning. But it
didn't *have* to be that way, Jemmy says. Back in Africa, he
knew somethin' different and he never let it go. And *we*
didn't have to either. I heard him say somethin' like 'The
enemy of my enemy is my friend.' He was talkin' 'bout the
Spanish down in Florida. Jemmy said if we struck out together, we could make it to St. Augustine."

Tiberius stared past his captors, his eyes narrowing a
little, watching something only he could see. "I never *thought*
about bein' free 'til then. Never *saw* how things could be different than they was until I listened to Jemmy. Everythin'
looked *changed* after he spoke. Like I'd lived alla my life in a
cave, believin' the shadows I seen were real until Jemmy held
up a light and they all melted away. For the first time I could
see what things would be like if the best food we had wasn't
leftovers from the mastah's plate, how I wouldn't need to tip
around all the time, peepin' and hidin' and worryin' 'bout
what white folks might be up to. What I'm sayin' is that if
you listened to Jemmy—*really* listened—you come to see that
slavery was mad. *Just mad.* We was all like folks in one of
them madhouses, black and white, thinkin' the way we
lived and died was the nat'ral ways of things when, from top
to bottom, it was crazy as can be. *We* were crazy. I felt like
a sleeper. A man who'd been dreamin' his whole life.
But Jemmy woke me hup. And when I looked at the men

Jemmy'd brought together, some of 'em wearin' old shoes fixed up with wire or no shoes at all, I seen they'd follow him anywhere."

From outside two rifle shots exploded, shattering the air. Tiberius stopped. Through the barn door he saw two militiamen dragging a black body across the yard. He stood up, taking a hesitant step toward the door. Ethan Whittaker shoved Tiberius back onto the barrel.

"Like I said, Jemmy swore he'd kill me if I told on 'em. I knew they was gonna break into the general store to steal arms and gunpowder, but I swear I didn't know they planned to kill Mr. Bathurst and Mr. Gibbs. Nossir. I let on like I was with 'em, but as soon as I could, I slipped away and come back to the house. I wanted freedom, you know, but I wasn't ready to kill nobody, 'least not on the Sabbath."

Tiberius began coughing from the smell of gunpowder drifting into the barn. Outside, every few moments another Negro was executed by the Carolina militia. He looked at the nearly empty bottle in Colonel Bull's hand and, panting a little, said, "You think I could whet my throat with some of that?" Bull stepped forward, grabbed Tiberius's hair in his left hand, and held the flask to the prisoner's lips with his right. Liquor ran down the sides of Tiberius's mouth. After his last swallow, he clamped shut his eyes as the home brew burned its way down. Then Tiberius sighed, and went on:

"So I knew what they was hup to, yessir. But I wasn't part of it, not at first. When I got to Mastah Boswell's house, it wasn't cold enough to start a fire, so I went right to the smokehouse and got some ham hanging from the rafters, then to the dairyhouse. I took all the fixin's for breakfast back to the kitchen. I didn't see Della. So I started makin' Mastah Boswell's breakfast myself. That took, oh, maybe two hours. Then, just as I was settin' the food on the table, I heard singin' outside. Thought I heard a drum too. Then the back door burst open. All of a sudden, I seen Jemmy and another fellah named Hannibal come flying barefoot through the dining room, so fast if I'd blinked I woulda missed 'em. Me, I stopped breathin'. I froze right where I was, butterin' a slice a toast, starin' at the ceilin' overhead. It was quiet, quiet, quiet. My head felt light. Didn't a sound breathe through that house until from hupstairs I heard a *thump*. Godamercy, they musta cut Mastah Boswell's throat straightaway. Next come his wife screaming. They took their time with her, playin' with her, I reckon. And since I didn't know what else to do—I mean, I was part of this thing now, whether I was ready or not—I sat down at the table, stuck a napkin under my collar, and commenced to eatin' that nice breakfast I put out before it got cold. I figure there wasn't no sense in it goin' to waste, right? 'Bout time I was finishin' my second cup of mint tea, Jemmy and Hannibal come downstairs, blood splattered over 'em like they been to a butcherin'. Hannibal was carryin' Mastah Boswell's head. He put it on the front porch like a Halloween pumpkin..."

Colonel Bull muttered something, then swung the butt of his gun against Tiberius's head, knocking him off the barrel. Hutchenson and Whittaker pulled him off the prisoner, who was bleeding now from a gash on his forehead. Hutchenson helped him back onto the barrel.

"Why'd you'd do that?" Tiberius's head was tucked like a turtle's. He asked Hutchenson, "Why'd he *do* that? I been tellin' the truth!" He watched them talking among themselves, whispering, and angrily brought out, "No, I'm *not* lyin'! What's that? What'd he say? Colonel Bull sayin' I tried to drag him off his horse? Oh, *that's* where I remember you from! Well sir, I...I ain't callin' you no liar, I wouldn't do *that*. I guess maybe me'n some of the others *did* pull a white man off his horse when he come ridin' down Pon Pon Road...but I just got swept hup in the rebellion, that's all."

They were quiet for a few moments. Hutchenson had that sad look on his face again. Colonel Bull began loading his rifle. Whittaker took a step toward Tiberius, who flinched, waiting to be hit again, but all the overseer did was ask a simple question.

"Nossir, Mistah Whittaker, I did *not* kill anybody. You know me better'n that. I wouldn't hurt a fly, sir. It's just that, like I was tryin' to tell you, I felt like I'd been sleepin' *all* my life and just woke hup. You a Christian man, right? You understand how it feels when the spirit hits you at meetin' time, like you was blind but suddenly you can see. That's how it was for me. I *was* with them when they left the farm, that's right, and marched over to the Godfrey place, then to the Lemy farm, pickin' up as they went more field hands ready to risk everythin' for just one day of freedom and folks like me, who wanted it too but was used to the old ways and had to be swept along. I reckon Jemmy had an army of over a hundred by the time y'all found our camp. We'd covered ten miles and Jemmy thought maybe he'd brought the whole Province to its knees. Guess that was a mistake, eh?" He tilted his head left to keep the blood trickling from his forehead out of his eyes. "I just want you to know the reason they let so many good white people live—the ones what treated colored folks right—is 'cause I took hup for 'em. That's right."

"That's enough," said Hutchenson. "You don't have to tell us any more. I understand. I believe in freedom, too." He lifted Tiberius to his feet, gripping his left arm. Whittaker took hold of his right. They began walking him toward the barn door.

"Thank you, Mr. Hutchenson," he said. "I *knew* you'd understand. I guess y'all fixin' to let me go now, huh?"

Poetry and Politics

"PHILLIS, HAVE YOU a moment to talk?"

"Of course, ma'am, but should you be up at this hour? The doctor said—"

"I *know* what he said. Pooh! You've been reminding me of it every day since you returned from England, which I wish you'd *not* done for my sake. I'm an old woman, and far poorer company, I would guess, than the Countess of Huntingdon and Benjamin Franklin. He isn't *really* a nudist, is he?"

"To hear others tell it, yes! I swear I heard them say it! And you're *not* poor company. I'd rather be here, helping you and Master John, than riding in carriages from one court to another in London and being called the 'Sable Muse.' Isn't that *silly*? I've never seen so many people astonished—there and here—that an Ethiop could write verse!"

"No, not an Ethiop. They're dazzled, and well should they be, at a girl barely thirteen translating Ovid from the Latin and publishing her first book at twenty. I daresay you are a prodigy, probably the most gifted poet in New England."

"Oh my…Better than Michael Wigglesworth?"

"Leagues beyond *him*, my dear."

"Perhaps you are…biased. Is that possible?"

"Not a'tall…"

"But Mr. Jefferson, his opinion of my work is less than laudatory."

"As is my opinion of him. Come now, show me what you're working on. That is a new poem, isn't it? Is that why you're up before cock's crow?"

"Oh, I couldn't sleep! But, no! Don't look! Give it back, *please*. I know it's not good. At least not yet. It could be years before it's ready—"

"I just want to see. May I? Well…this *is* a departure for you. 'On the Necessity of Negro Manumussion.' What prompted you to begin this?"

"You…and Master John."

"How so?"

"Just prior to sending me to London for medical treatment you granted me manumission—"

"We were worried. Your health has always been frail."

"—and when I was there I discovered that everyone of my color was free. Just a few months before I arrived, Chief Justice Mansfield passed a ruling that freed all the slaves in England. I was thinking, would that we had such a ruling here!"

"But there *are* free black men and women in Boston."

"Yes, and they live miserably, ma'am! My contact with

them is slight, but I've seen them languishing in poverty and ostracized by white Christians. I wonder sometimes what they think of *me*. I imagine some mock the models I've chosen—Alexander Pope—and my piety and the patriotism of my verse, such as the poem to General Washington, which you know I labored long and hard upon, though he is a slaveholder (and who replied not at all to my gift), so that, the *hardest* work sometimes, at least for me, has been to honor in my verse the principles of the faith that brought me freedom, yet—and yet—I have not spoken of its failures, here in New England or in the slaveholding states that justify my people's oppression by twisting scripture."

"Must you speak of these things?"

"Yes, I think so..."

"Is this why you could not sleep last night?"

"Yes, ma'am."

"Phillis...are you...unhappy here?"

"No, no! That's *not* what I'm saying. I'm thankful for the blessing that brought me from Senegal to America. Thankful that you took on the sickly child that I was, carried me here to be a companion for you, taught me to write and read, and introduced me to Horace and Virgil, associates with whom I can spend hours, and ne'er once have they rebuked me for my complexion—"

"The finest thoughts have no complexion."

"So I have believed, ma'am. I believe that *still*. But while the greatest thoughts and works of literature and the gatekeepers of heaven vouchsafe no distinctions based on color, the *worst* prejudices and passions of man reign throughout the colonies. Will it not be odd, a hundred years hence, when readers open *Poems on Various Subjects, Religious and Moral* by Phillis Wheatley, and discover that in not a single poem do I address the anguish of bondage, the daily horror that is happening around us, the evil of men bleeding their sable brethren for profit? Will I not be *suspect*? Or censured? For it is our hope—isn't it?—that freedom will come to all? If it does, ma'am, what will free Negroes think of me? That I wrote nothing to further our cause?"

"Would you become a pamphleteer then? A writer of newspaper articles?"

"Well, no, but—"

"And *why* not a pamphleteer?"

"It's obvious why, isn't it? At the end of the day one wraps garbage in newspapers. And while a pamphlet can be valuable and stir people to action, a hundred years hence it may be forgotten—as the injustice it assails is forgotten—or it will be preserved only as a historical document, interesting for what it reveals about a moment long past, but *never* appreciated as art. I'm speaking of writing *poems* about oppression."

"Is poetry the right means for that?"

"How do you mean?"

"Tell me, Phillis, what is it about Virgil, Pope, and Horace that you love? Come now, don't be shy."

"The beauty, which age does not wear—"

"And?"

"The truth…"

"Which is timeless, no?"

"Yes, that's right."

"May I suggest something?"

"Please."

"I cannot read tea leaves so I have no idea what the future will bring or how your poetry will be received in the colonies a century from now. But of one thing I can assure you: You can never be censured. You are the first internationally celebrated woman poet in the colonies. The first American poet of your people. I'm sure they will take pride in your achievement, as John and I do. And you, my dear, are—by nature and temperament—a poet, regardless of what Jefferson says. You are not a pamphleteer. Your job is simple. I did not say *easy*, for no one knows better than you how difficult it is to create even *one* line of verse worth passing along to the next generation, or a poem that speaks to the heart of Christendom—white and colored—on both sides of the Atlantic. It is a noble calling, Phillis, this creating of beauty, and it is sufficient unto itself."

"Is it? Sometimes I wonder if my people see me—my work—as useless."

"Useless?"

"It doesn't *serve* their liberation, does it?"

"Why? Because you do not catalog horrors? Only praise what on these shores is praiseworthy?"

"Yes, exactly."

"Dear, dear Phillis..."

"Why are you laughing? What did I say? Am I amusing?"

"Oh no, of course not! But would you call Benjamin Banneker's work useless?"

"Hardly! While still a boy, he built from wood the first clock made wholly in America. From what I hear, it keeps perfect time to this very day."

"What, then, of Santomee?"

"Who?"

"He was a slave in New York, one trained in Holland, who practiced medicine among the Dutch and English, probably saving many lives. And there is Onesimus, who in 1721 came up with an antidote for the smallpox. All of them proved the genius of your people. All of them enriched others through their deeds, thereby providing in the example of their persons, and the universal value of their products, the most devastating broadside against the evils of Negro bondage imaginable. And you have done no less."

"You think so?"

"I *know* so."

"Thank you, ma'am. You are most kind."

"Will you continue, then, with this bristling, new poem?"

"Perhaps, if I can find my way into it. The *problem* is not that I don't feel outrage whenever I read or see or hear of injustice, it's rather that I fear I have no real talent for that sort of writing and rhetoric. For things I hate. I think I can compose passably well a hymn to morning, but as soon as I turn my pen to painting a portrait of a slave suffering beneath the lash, I cut myself off from what flows most easily from me—the things I love—and the words fall woodenly, unconvincingly, onto the page."

"No, it's not your best work."

"You're not supposed to *say* that!"

"Sorry! I was just agreeing with you, that's all. You needn't bite my head off!"

"You're supposed to tell me it's good."

"Fine, it's good."

"You don't *mean* that."

"You're right, I don't, but I'm in no mood for an argument before breakfast. And it's not why I wanted to talk to you."

"Why did you?"

"You know how yesterday I felt poorly and stayed in bed?"

"Yes?"

"Well, I didn't bother with the post. All the mail, scented and sealed with candle wax, sat on a wig stand until I awoke this morning. I began looking through it, and I found a letter addressed to you. Perhaps I shouldn't give it to you if you're planning now on starting a new life as a composer of pamphlets."

"Oh, please! Who is it from?"

"Phillis, I think you should sit down."

"*Who?*"

"May I read it to you?"

"*I* can read!"

"But I would enjoy it so!"

"All right, then! Read!"

"Ahem…

*"Miss Phillis,
Your favor of the 26th of October did not reach my hands till*

the middle of December. Time enough, you will say, to have given an answer ere this. Granted. But a variety of important occurances, continually interposing to distract the mind and withdraw the attention, I hope will apologize for the delay, and plead my excuse for the seeming but not real neglect. I thank you most sincerely for your polite notice of me, in the elegant lines you enclosed; and however undeserving I may be of such encomium and panegyric, the style and manner exhibit a striking proof of your poetical talents; in honor of which, and as a tribute justly due to you, I would have published the poem, had I not been apprehensive that, while I only meant to give the world this new instance of your genius, I might have incurred the imputation of vanity. This, and nothing else, determined me not to give it place in the public prints.... If you should ever come to Cambridge, or near headquarters, I shall be happy to see a person so favored by the Muses, and to whom nature has been so liberal and beneficent in her dispensations. I am, with great respect...

> *Your obedient, humble servant,*
> *George Washington"*

"He said...*servant?*"
"Here, see for yourself."
"This a complicated time, isn't it?"
"Yes, dear, I think it is."

A Soldier for the Crown

YOU ALWAYS WERE a gambler.

Before the war broke out, when you were still a servant in Master William Selby's house, you'd bet on anything—how early spring thaw might come, or if your older brother Titus would beat your cousin Caesar in a wrestling match—and most of the time you won. There was something about gambling that you could not resist. There was suspense, the feeling that the future was not already written by white hands. Or finished. There was chance, the luck of the draw. In the roll of dice or a card game, there was always—what to call it?—an *openness*, a chance that the outcome would go this way or that. For or against you. Of course, in bondage to Master Selby there were no odds. Whichever way the dice fell or the cards came up, you began and ended your day a slave.

But did you win *this* time?

Standing by the wooden rail on a ship bound for Nova Scotia, crammed with strangers fleeing the collapse of their colonial world—women and children, whites and blacks, whose names appear in Brigadier General Samuel Birch's *Book of Negroes*—you pull a long-shanked pipe from your red-tinted coat, pack the bowl with tobacco, and strike a friction match against a nail in your bootheel. You know you are fortunate to be on board. Now that the Continental Army is victorious, blacks who fought for the crown are struggling desperately to leave on His Majesty's ships departing from New York harbor. Even as your boat eased away from the harbor, some leaped from the docks into the water, swimming toward the ship for this last chance to escape slavery. Seeing them, you'd thought, *That might have been me.* But it wasn't; you've always been lucky that way, at taking risks. Running away from bondage. Taking on new identities. Yet you wonder what to call yourself now. A loyalist? A traitor? A man without a country? As the harbor shrinks, growing fainter in the distance, severing you forever from this strange, newly formed nation called the United States, you haven't the slightest idea after years of war which of these names fits, or what the future holds, though on one matter you *are* clear:

From the start, you were fighting for no one but yourself.

The day after Lieutenant General Sir Henry Clinton promised liberty to all blacks deserting the rebel standard and willing to fight on the side of the British, you learned that Titus and Caesar were planning to flee. In the evening, on your way to the quarters after finishing your duties in the house, Titus stopped you outside the barn, and asked, "Can you go back to the kitchen and sneak out some provisions

for us?" Naturally, you'd asked him what for, and he put his
fingers to his lips, shushing you. They planned to steal two
horses, he said. Then ride to safety behind British lines.
"You're leaving?" You were almost speechless with anger.
"And you're not taking *me*?"

"How can I?" he asked. "You're only fifteen."

"What's that got to do with anything? I can fight!"

"You ever fired a gun?"

"No, but I can learn!"

"Once I'm free, and got the papers to prove it, I'll come
back."

"Titus, if you don't take me, I'll *tell*."

For a heartbeat or two, Titus looked as if he might hit
you. Grudgingly, he agreed to bring you along, despite your
age and his declaration after your parents' deaths that he'd
keep you from harm. You did as he requested, returning to
the house and filling a sack with food, Master Selby's clothing, even some of the mistress's jewelry that the three of you
might barter, then delivered all this to your brother and
Caesar in the barn. The three of you left that night on two
of the master's best horses, you riding behind Titus, your
arms tightly circling his waist until you stopped to make
camp in the woods. There, Caesar suggested that it would
help if you all changed your names and appearances as
much as possible since Master Selby was sure to post your
descriptions. Titus said fine, he'd grow a beard and call himself John Free. Caesar liked that, said, "Then I'll be George
Liberty." They waited for you to pick a name, poking sticks
at the campfire, sending up sparks into the starless sky.

"Give me time," you'd said, changing into buckskin breeches, blue stockings, and a checkered, woolen shirt. "I'll shave my hair off, and I'll think of *something* before we get there. I don't want to rush." What you didn't tell them that night was how thrilling, how sweet this business of renaming oneself felt, and that you wanted to toy with a thousand possibilities—each name promising a new nature—turning them over on your tongue, and creating whole histories for each before settling, as you finally did, on "Alexander Freeman"as your new identity.

Thus, it was Alexander Freeman, George Liberty, and John Free who rode a few days later, bone weary from travel, into the British camp. You will never forget this sight: scores of black men in British uniforms, with the inscription LIBERTY TO SLAVES on their breasts, bearing arms so naturally one would have thought they were born with a rifle in their hands. Some were cleaning their weapons. Others marched. Still others were relaxing or stabbing their bayonets at sacks suspended from trees or performing any of the thousand chores that kept a regiment well-oiled and ready. When you signed on, the black soldier who wrote down your names didn't question you, though he remarked he thought you didn't look very strong. The three of you were put immediately to work. Harder work, you recall, than anything you'd known working in Master Selby's house, but for the first time in fifteen years you fell to each task eagerly, gambling that the labor purchased a new lease on life.

Over the first months, then years of the seesawing war, you, Titus, and Caesar served His Majesty's army in more capacities than you had fingers on the hand: as orderlies to the white officers, laborers, cooks, foragers, and as foot soldiers who descended upon farms abandoned by their white owners, burning the enemy's fortifications and plundering plantations for much-needed provisions; as spies slipping in and out of southern towns to gather information; and as caretakers to the dying when smallpox swept through your regiment, weakening and killing hundreds of men. Your brother among them. And it was then you nearly gave up the gamble. You wondered if it might not be best to take your chips off the table. And pray the promise of the Virginia Convention that black runaways to the British side would be pardoned was genuine. And slink back home, your hat in your hand, to Master Selby's farm—if it was still there. Or perhaps you and Caesar might switch sides, deserting to the ranks of General Washington who, pressured for manpower, belatedly reversed his opposition to Negroes fighting in the Continental Army. And then there was that magnificent Declaration penned by Jefferson, proclaiming that "We hold these truths to be self-evident, that all men are created equal, that they are endowed by their Creator with certain unalienable Rights, that among these are Life, Liberty and the pursuit of Happiness," words you'd memorized after hearing them. If the Continentals won, would this brave, new republic be so bad?

"Alex, those are just *words*," said Caesar. "White folks' words for other white folks."

"But without us, the rebels would lose—"

"So would the redcoats. Both sides need us, but I don't

trust neither one to play fair when this thing is over. They can do that Declaration over. Naw, the words I want to see are on a British pass with my name on it. I'm stayin' put 'til I see *that*."

Caesar never did. A month later your regiment was routed by the Continental Army. The rebels fired cannons for six hours, shelling the village your side occupied two days before. You found pieces of your cousin strewn everywhere. And you ran. Ran. You lived by your wits in the countryside, stealing what you needed to survive until you reached territory still in British hands, and again found yourself a pawn in the middle of other men's battles—Camden, where your side scattered poorly trained regulars led by General Gates, then liberated slaves who donned their masters' fancy clothing and powdered wigs and followed along behind Gates as his men pressed on; and the disastrous encounter at Guilford Court House, where six hundred redcoats died and Cornwallis was forced to fall back to Wilmington for supplies, then later abandon North Carolina altogether, moving on to Virginia. During your time as a soldier, you saw thousands sacrifice their lives, and no, it wasn't as if you came through with only a scratch. At Camden you took a ball in your right shoulder. Fragments remain there still, making it a little hard for you to sleep on that side or withstand the dull ache in your shoulder on days when the weather is damp. But, miraculously, as the war began to wind down, you were given the elusive, long-coveted British pass.

On the ship, now traveling north past Augusta, you knock your cold pipe against the railing, shaking dottle from its bowl, then reach into your coat for the scrap of paper that was so difficult to earn. Behind you, other refugees are bedding down for the night, covering themselves and their children with blankets. You wait until one of the hands on deck passes a few feet beyond where you stand, then you unfold the paper with fingers stiffened by the cold. In the yellowish glow of the ship's lantern, tracing the words with your forefinger, shaping your lips silently to form each syllable, you read:

> This is to certify to whomfoever it may concern, that the Bearer hereof ...Alexander Freeman...a Negro, reforted to the Britifh Lines, in confequence of the Proclamations of Sir William Howe, and Sir Henry Clinton, late Commanders in Chief in America; and that the faid Negro has hereby his Excellency Sir Benjamin Hampton's Permiffion to go to Nova-Scotia, or wherever elfe he may think proper...By Order of Brigadier General Ruttledge

The document, dated April 1783, brings a broad smile to your lips. Once your ship lands, and you find a home, you will frame this precious deed of manumission. At least in this sense, your gamble paid off. And for now you still prefer the adopted name Alexander Freeman to the one given you at birth—Dorothy.

Maybe you'll be Dorothy again, later in Nova Scotia. Of course, you'll keep the surname Freeman. And, Lord willing, when it's safe you will let your hair grow out again to its full length, wear dresses, and perhaps start a new family to replace the loved ones you lost during the war.

Martha's Dilemma

NOTHING HAS BEEN quite the same since George's funeral, including his Negroes. I've been managing the affairs at Mount Vernon, as I always did when he was away, first during the Revolution, then when they kept calling him back to a government service he never truly felt equal to, nurturing the fledging nation that is, I suppose, the child we never had. But even as I devote my days to managing this sprawling estate, particularly instructing the servants to maintain the arcade connecting the house to our workshops and greenhouses, of which he was so proud, I cannot help but think about how little time we had together after the Old Man turned in his resignation at the Philadelphia State House. Two years! They passed so quickly, and much of it was consumed by his entertaining visitors from all over the world when he wasn't laboring—with those nice, two young men he hired—to keep up with voluminous correspondence. And even then that owlish old curmudgeon John Adams had the nerve to ask him out of retirement to help refine the military when Talleyrand tried to blackmail us for the right of Yankee ships to have free passage on the seas, knowing—as Adams always knew—that George could never say no, that he'd struggle into his old uniform and leave for Philadelphia to once again transform pitifully unprepared farmer-soldiers into fighting men for a new republic. If he'd only known how sick the Old Man was sometimes; I doubt Adams realized, despite his being right there, that on Inauguration Day, by the time George reached the balcony of the Federal Building, where he would place his hand on the Bible and become president, he was so ill he collapsed onto the first chair he found.

Yes, they were careless with him, his admirers—I *always* told him that. But he was careless with himself, too, believing perhaps in his own indestructibility after his surveying work on the Virginia frontier, that dreadful winter at Valley Forge, the illnesses he'd overcome during the Revolution before he was even aware that he was ill, and having two horses shot out from under him in the midst of terrible gunfire during the French and Indian War. On December 13 I gave him a good piece of my mind about that, when he returned from riding on a day as dreary and damp as any I've seen. Naturally, he waved off my objections, "Oh, it's not all that bad outside, Martha," but he was shivering and sneezing when the servants took his wraps. At dinner, he barely touched his food. When he spoke I could tell his voice was getting stuffy. That he had the beginnings of a bad cold, and here we were so close to the holidays—and just after George's nephew Lawrence married Nellie Custis—with so many people on our social calendar to see! Oh, I scolded him severely, the big oaf, and sent him off to bed, to which he shyly retreated with a rum and toddy.

I should have *known* something was wrong.

Two hours later when I climbed under the covers, kissing him on his cheek, I discovered he had no voice at all. He couldn't talk. I rang the bell for Billy Lee, one of our most trustworthy servants, and when he arrived, breathless after running from the kitchen, I told him to saddle a horse immediately and ride to Dr. James Craik's home nearby, and to fetch him, regardless if he'd turned in for the night or not. Poor George could only communicate with me in writing. He took a quill, paper, and ink from his study, smiled at me, and scrawled, *Not to worry, James will fix me up. If he forces me to stay in bed, do remember to have someone see to the lame horse I told you about, and take care of the washout in the fields.*

Dr. Craik, an old friend, arrived just before midnight. He examined the Old Man, and then looked very grave. Turning to me, he said, "Lady Washington, your husband has a severe case of quinsy. That's an inflammation of the tonsils," he explained, though I knew perfectly well what quinsy was and felt a little miffed by his condescension, but this is a cross women have had to bear from time immemorial, that and living in the shadow of their spouses, of course. He recommended, as was right, that Billy ride all night to Alexandria (By Billy's crabbed expression at this chore I should have seen a portent of things to come) to bring two physicians of his acquaintance to help with cupping the Old Man, which our servant did. The next day Dr. Craik and those two men he'd summoned bled George. I was by his bedside all the while, holding his piebald hand firmly, and I must say that it is to Billy's credit that he never left my side except to jump to any task or errand that Dr. Craik asked of him. Our house servants waited solemnly outside the door, whispering among themselves, in part because I believe they loved the Old Man, and in greater part because all had heard that upon his (and my) death their manumission was promised in our will. They too were godsent that day. They saw to the chores I was too distracted to discharge, some prayed for my husband's swift recovery, and others wept. Nevertheless, all our ministrations came to nought. At ten o'clock on December 14, 1799, the man with whom I'd shared life for forty years—since our wedding when we both were twenty-seven—went on to his reward.

What, I have been wondering, is *my* reward, now that he's gone?

All over this new country he served indefatigably, flags were lowered when word of his death went abroad. In America's churches, state assemblies, and the government he'd created, there were eulogies, the finest of them coming from Harry Lee—known as "Light Horse Harry" when he served under George during the Revolution—who said my husband was "First in war, first in peace, and first in the hearts of his countrymen." These were beautiful tributes, for which I am thankful. I can even turn an appreciative, albeit amused, smile toward the well-meaning mythmakers who began enlarging his legend before we could properly bury him in Mount Vernon's family tomb, spinning outrageous tales of his throwing a silver dollar across the Rappahannock River

(What balderdash!), and that when his father, Augustine, discovered one of his cherry trees cut down, young George confessed to the deed, saying, "I cannot tell a lie." Well, I can tell you this: No one knew the Old Man as well as I did. He could lie, oh yes. He was, after all, a *politician*. Oh, and if one could see his temper when he was angry! Like Vesuvius, that was. Nor did he have the Olympian self-confidence so many attributed to him, what with the paucity of his education. He was painfully shy with every girl before he met me, possibly because his face bore scars from the smallpox he endured while journeying as a boy with his half-brother Lawrence to the West Indies. He was a slow reader. A poor speller. He was a man of deeds, not ideas. He knew no French at all and thus signed a miserable terms of surrender when he was captured during the battle of Great Meadows. Those are matters I assisted him with—matters of culture—as well as adding five thousand acres to his estate when we wed—indeed, you could say it was seventeen thousand acres, if you count the land now owned by my son. No, he was not perfect, but what woman could have asked for a better companion for these last forty years?

When I was a very young girl, studying the classics, I read that the ancient Greeks honored their Olympic game heroes by knocking out a portion of the wall that protected their city—the heroes stood in that spot for the rest of the day, the idea being that with champions such as them a wall was not needed. On December 14 it felt across this country, and especially at Mount Vernon, that we had lost not only a hero but one of the very foundations of our house. For days after his passing I spoke to no one about the depth of this absence save to my dearest and closest friends. Nor did I speak of how subtly I began to see a change in our servants. At first, I thought the smiles with which they greeted me were simply intended to cheer me a little. Then, ever so slowly, I realized they were smiling too much. And too often. Sometimes when I started to enter the kitchen, I'd stop outside the door, listening to the blacks laughing whilst they prepared my meals, and once our cook told the chambermaid how pleased she was that now she'd never again have to slave all day to prepare the elaborate desserts the Old Man was so fond of. At that point, I strode inside. Seeing me, both women went fussily back to work, ducking their heads, but I saw one of them, I swear, wink at the other.

Strangely enough, the worst among them was Billy Lee. With my husband dead and buried, he started behaving as if *he* was now the master of Mount Vernon, or at least over the other servants. This would have been impossible, I realized, had George and I not become so dependent upon the blacks. We'd delegated so many household responsibilities to them, and not just in the manor but in the tobacco fields as well, that I would be at pains to tell you the inventory of our kitchen, or how well the Old Man's latest agricultural experiments were proceeding. Ironically, we were enslaved to *them*, shackled to their industry, the knowledge they'd acquired because we were too busy running the country to develop it ourselves!

One afternoon last week Billy brought me my tea as I was writing thank-you notes to those many people who'd sent me condolences. He actually *pointed* his dark finger at me, wagged it, and said, "Lady Washington, you should let them scribes the master hired do that." I mean, he was telling *me* what I should do. More than once I sniffed our best brandy on his breath. I heard him *swearing* at a stable hand, and do you think he was at all ashamed when I chastised him? Hardly!

It was, then, perhaps a month after the Old Man's death, that I began to fear the Negroes who resided in every nook and cranny of my life. At night, from their quarters, I began to hear drums, which George had expressly forbidden them to play. Food began to disappear from our pantries. Many of our plants died in the greenhouse from neglect. And there I was, an old woman still grieving over the love of her youth, surrounded on all sides by George's slaves who knew that when *I* expired they were free. (My own servants we had not yet decided about.) Privately, with me and friends, my husband declared his repugnance for slavery. He knew it was wrong. And hoping to right that wrong—one he'd known as a slave master since his eleventh year—he built liberation for his Negroes after my death into his last will and testament. (No, I was not thoroughly consulted on this matter.) And by doing so, he created the most frightening prison for *me*.

I am afraid to be alone in any room in my house with Billy Lee, given the way I sometimes catch him looking at me out of the corner of his eye. My Lord, I am afraid to *eat*, for anything they serve me might be poisoned. It chills me to hear the footsteps of any of our servants behind me when

I am on the stairs, or outside my bedroom door at night. Oh, George, you were *not* a thinker. Had you been, you would not out of Christian kindness to the blacks unwittingly consigned me to a hellish house, where in the face of each of our formerly loving attendants I now see my possible executioner.

How many days, or weeks, I have lived in this agony, I do not know. How long I have to live after my dear husband's departure is also a mystery. But I awoke this morning with a clear resolve. I bade one of the black children to have our coachman ready the carriage to take me in a few moments to Fairfax County court. There, I will sign the papers necessary to release from servitude all of George's Negroes. They must be manumitted now. This very afternoon.

Then, and only then, will they and I be free of the errors of George Washington.

The Plague

JULY 5, 1793
FRIDAY, 8:30 P.M.

    I have kept this journal for a few months now, initially to document for posterity the early work I am doing to open—soon, I hope—the doors of a church I will call Bethel, but as we now enter the second (or perhaps it is the third) month of deaths due to the yellow fever, I wonder if it might be more appropriate to title these pages *The Plague Journal*.

    Death is all around us, like a biblical parable on (white) vanity. Should I make that the subject of my five o'clock sermon tomorrow morning? I wonder how it might be received? Perhaps well, insofar as my congregation is entirely Cainite—so white men call us—the colored outcasts violently driven from St. George's, one of Philadelphia's largest Methodist churches just last year. I know in the eyes of God, the behavior of this city's Abelites was scandalous. We, free men and women, came humbly to their church to pray to the Creator. Rev. Absalom Jones and I were a little late. Without causing any noise or commotion whatsoever, we quickly went up the stairs of St. George to the newly built gallery, which was just above the seats we'd occupied the week before. The strains of the first hymn were ending as we sat down, then the church elder told all those present to pray. Obediently, we got down on our knees. But hardly was I a minute into silent meditation when at my right I heard Absalom make a sound. Opening my eyes, I saw one of St. George's trustees hauling my companion to his feet, telling him Negroes were never, never, never to sit in this section of the gallery. Naturally, my friends and I left, turning our backs on all of Philadelphia's white churches. One Sabbath after the next we were subjected to humiliations it pains me to remember. Good Christians, for example, who refused to take the sacrament if it meant sipping from the same chalice that had touched the lips of their darker brethren. Oh yes, Absalom was compelled to organize St. Thomas Episcopal Church after that sad incident, and I dream of a ground-breaking ceremony someday at Bethel, that we might better separate ourselves from those who reject us, and all of this simply that we can worship our common Father in the spirit He intended.

Yet now, ironically, He has visited upon this city's whites a plague of medieval proportions. It is a swift disease. It can kill in a single day. Week by week, the death toll mounts. Frightened whites flee this capital city of Philadelphia by the thousands, abandoning their families and friends. Those who remain are helpless in the grip of this growing malignancy, for the country's government is paralyzed. The crisis is unparalleled in this country's history. But word has spread that Negroes are immune to the disease, which is not true, of course. Nonetheless, the Abelites believe we are protected, and so Dr. Benjamin Rush, knowing of the leadership position I occupy through God's grace among my own people, has appealed to me to plead with them to assist the city's remaining civic leaders in combating the curse that is laying them low.

I prayed—and prayed—on his proposal. And in the midst of my appeal to the Most High for guidance, I remembered the injunction, "Bear ye one another's burdens, and so fulfill the law of Christ" (Galatians 6:2). This crisis, the Lord let me see, is possibly our invitation as a people back from our exile east of Eden. If we help the Abelites in their hour of need, mightn't they be thankful to the Negroes of Philadelphia? Wouldn't their hatred be replaced by gratitude? Such has been my hope since I enlisted my people in the dangerous work of saving others who have long despised them.

JULY 21, 1793
SUNDAY, 6 P.M.

Preached four sermons today in the Commons, in Southwark, and Northern Liberties, and as always after such a day I feel a bit emotionally drained, yet also exhilarated, so I know it will be difficult to fall asleep at my usual hour of 9 P.M. But do *I* preach? It seems more fitting to say that when I stand before my people, the Book in my left hand, the words come flooding out of me, as if I were merely a conduit, an anonymous instrument through which the music of our Lord and Savior bursts forth. Afterwards, it's true, I cannot recall everything I said, though the laity always seem pleased and tell me that I am good. No, I've told them time again, not I but the Father within me doeth the works, and I ask them to read Matthew 19:17.

However, that glow that comes after a day of sermonizing lasted no longer than it took for me to step back onto the streets of Philadelphia and begin my walk home. The dead lie in ditches alongside the roads. I saw a white child who was crying, wandering about like a phantom because she has the plague and her parents turned her out into the street. They did not want her to infect the rest of their family. Yellow fever is no respecter of age, color, sex, caste, or social position—the doctors are dying just as swiftly as their patients, which reminds me that I must look in on Dr. Benjamin Rush, a good and decent white man, and a true Abolitionist.

Note: My businesses need attention.

One other thing about this plague troubles me. God does nothing, we know, without having a purpose in mind. We cannot, of course, fathom His will entirely, though my hope, as I've written, is that this affliction will soften the hearts of whites to the Negroes laboring to help them. But is there a deeper message in this sickness that has befallen Philadelphia like the Flood, or locusts darkening the sky? I have taken this question each day into my mid-afternoon meditation, but as of yet I have no answer.

AUGUST 6, 1793
TUESDAY, 5:20 P.M.

Spent this morning digging a common grave outside the city for burying the dead, which we loaded onto wagons at 6 A.M. Three of my congregation and I rode slowly up one street, down another, shouting, "Bring out your dead." Which six people did, dragging the corpses from their homes, then pitching them onto our wagon. As we bore them out of town, I looked back at their bodies. They were heaped together like broken dolls. Their flesh was yellow. Already two of them had gone ripe. The other three were more recently dead, their limbs stiff as boards. In that pile of putrefying flesh I saw—or thought I saw—the trustee from St. George's, the one who'd expelled Absalom and myself. I believe it was him, but the decomposition of his face made a definite identification difficult.

He had not wanted me in his church, or touching him. As things turned out, once we had dug a hole six feet deep and wrapped the fetid corpses in sackcloth, my black hands were the last ones in this world to touch him. We shoveled dirt onto the bodies, and when I could no longer see the trustee's face—which, God forgive me, I hated—I said a brief prayer that all their souls might wing heavenward, though should that doubtful event happen, I'm sure the trustee would be standing at the gate when I arrived, telling Jesus that my black brethren and I should not be admitted.

But I prayed for him, yes. And for myself (11 Timothy 2:1–3), for the removal of my anger. For does not the Light of the World tell us that we must forgive seven times seventy, if need be?

AUGUST 12, 1793
MONDAY, 8:45 P.M.

Just returned from making my rounds to the sick. Walked this morning at approximately 7 A.M. into the palatial home of a woman well known in Philadelphia for the lavish parties she holds in her ballroom. Everywhere my gaze fell I saw wealth. A chandelier, for example, that would pay for the building of ten Bethels. Furniture imported from France. I am certain this woman does not dwell often on Matthew 6:27, where it is written, "Which of you by taking thought can add one cubit unto his stature?" Her servant, a colored girl in my congregation, led me up the quarter-turn stairs to the woman's bedroom, where she lay semiconscious, emaciated as a skeleton. I could tell the disease was far along with her. Most likely, she was bleeding internally. Most of her golden hair—now stiff as straw—had fallen out onto her pillow. I began unpacking the apothecary case Dr. Rush had given me, laying out glass vials of various medicines, the little weighing scale, and instruments necessary for cupping. The old woman began to rouse. Seeing me, that I was a Negro—and one in her bedroom no less—she began to scream, shouting, *"Get out! Get out!"*

I repacked my case and promptly left. I did not plead with her or beg for the opportunity to save her life so that she could begin plans for her next party. Later in the day, through her servant girl, I was informed of her passing at

4 P.M. Perhaps God has sent this plague for the same reason His wrath destroyed Sodom. To cleanse our city of human corruption...

SEPTEMBER 1, 1793
SUNDAY, 7:00 P.M.

I have been ill, feverish for the last few weeks. Unable to write in addition to my other duties. It is not true that the plague bypasses people of color. For our numbers in Philadelphia, as many Negroes have perished as whites. What, then, heavenly Father, do you want us to learn from unending devastation?

EPTEMBER 12, 1793
THURSDAY, 4:18 P.M.

As I promised him, I again visited earlier this afternoon with Dr. Benjamin Rush, and as always our time together was uplifting. I cannot condemn white people precisely because I know someone like the good doctor. From the beginning he supported our black agents of mercy during this epidemic, and he could have fled Philadelphia along with the reportedly twenty thousand others who have abandoned the city, but being a true physician, and man of God, he remained during these months when his services were most needed.

I was discouraged to see, however, that the yellow pallor was upon his face this afternoon. He looked feverish, weakened by his own bout with the disease, and so I begged him not to stand, as he was struggling to do, when I entered his parlor. Slowly, he settled back against the cushions, perspiration beading along his brow, and tried to smile. He gave me the intelligence—blessed to hear—that across Philadelphia there were signs that the fever was beginning to abate. Fewer cases had been reported this week than the week previous. "Then we are winning?" I asked, too soon. "And when this is over, the citizens of this city will acknowledge the role played in its restoration by Negroes?" Dr. Rush looked down. His eyes narrowed. He gave a great, sad sigh, and said, "Would that were so, Richard, but already I am hearing the opposite of what we'd hoped. Rather than singing your people's praises, white men and women are saying blacks used the plague for their own profit. They tell me reports that Negroes stole when, in the guise of nurses, they entered white homes—and like vultures pilfered the bodies of the dead. Some have been accused of murdering, not saving, others. And even you, my friend, are being accused." I asked him of what, and he replied that many believed I was pocketing money because in the past week or two I was obliged to charge for some of the labors my people performed. I explained that it was true. We *were* asking for some remuneration, but only because we had exhausted all the volunteers who stepped forward to give freely of their time, and so I was forced to hire five men to assist me. The doctor nodded, "Oh, *I* believe you, and I will tell *every*one what you have told me. But I doubt it will change many of their hearts. In that case of medicines I gave you, there are many potions and elixirs for curing the ailments of the flesh.

I wish to God we could invent something for curing the sickness in the white soul."

So he spoke. I thanked him, then took my leave.

OCTOBER 16, 1793
WEDNESDAY, 9:50 P.M.

Unable to sleep, I walked the streets for long hours after dark this evening, and at every alleyway, park, and corner I came to, where the sick huddled round a fire, or wild dogs nibbled the flesh off a dead man's fingers, I saw a *memento mori*. A reminder that Dr. Rush and I had been foolish to believe the hearts of (white) men might ever change in the Earthly City. No, our salvation awaits only in that house not made by hands, eternal in the heavens. Wandering tonight after another day of delivering five sermons, I did see signs that the yellow fever was lessening its grip upon the city. I mused that perhaps soon that plague would be gone. Things would be as they were before. I stepped through now-healing white neighborhoods, ones I'd delivered medicines to only a month ago; I saw lily-white faces glaring at me through the windows, twisted lips drawn down in disgust at my very presence, and I knew at last, and with the certainty of revelation, that the exoteric lesson the good Lord wanted me to see was that, despite the best efforts by men of goodwill, some plagues never end.

A Report from St. Domingue

SIR,

I beg that you will forgive me for the inordinate lapse between this letter and my last. As I mentioned in that hasty missive of 4 July 1801, my initial meeting with Governor-General François-Dominique Toussaint went poorly. No, I mustn't lie. It was, Mr. President, a disaster of diplomacy, with Toussaint being haughtily unimpressed by my credentials, despite my previous work in President Washington's administration. He strutted about his chamber with the air of a Coriolanus, and all but looked down his nose at me (You know this expression of disdain—it is thoroughly French), asking why I had not brought from Monticello a personal greeting from you, for he fancies himself to be a freedom fighter like yourself; he insisted repeatedly that I must have misplaced such an important item of protocol; then he summarily postponed any further meetings with me

In this letter our consul is fictitious (Thomas Jefferson, in fact, sent Tobias Lear to represent him), but his fears are real.

until I found it. I daresay, it would have helped matters considerably if you had, in fact, written such a letter, though I understand your refusal to acknowledge in any way whatsoever (or treat as an equal head of state) St. Domingue's governor-general and the bloody Revolution he and his cohorts Jacques Dessalines and Henri Christophe have created on what was once the richest European colonial possession.

But, as I say, it was my intention to write you much earlier concerning your plan to help Bonaparte re-establish Gallic rule and Negro slavery on this sea-girt island. And I would have done so, I assure you, had not your consul gotten off to such a bad start, and then found such difficulty acclimating himself and his family to the extremes of this savage post to which you have assigned him. My health has been exceedingly tender. During the day the temperature here is well nigh 95 degrees. My French, as you know, is flawless, but most of the people I meet speak *Creole* French: a blend of Indian, French, and Spanish that I must at times strain my ears to decipher. In addition to this taxing problem of translating their native tongue, the food is unfamiliar; the favorite dish is a rice-and-bean concoction called *pois ac duriz colles*, which the natives wash down with rum and *tafia*, a head-ruining spirit made from sugarcane. Gastronomically, this diet of Negro dishes for the past several weeks has wreaked havoc with my digestion, that of my wife, and especially my eight-year-old son, Cornelius, who suffers from borborygm and stomach cramps, as do I, though if the truth be known, I suspect our physical distress has a darker cause, which I will try to summon the courage to speak of shortly.

Yet all that, Mr. President, is nothing compared to the *fear*.

To a man, the natives of St. Domingue believe in voodoo. During the nights of sweltering heat, when one's bedsheets are soaked through before dawn, we can hear from our lodgings in the capital the endless pounding of drums—the same tom-toms that one heard on August 22, 1791, when the voodoo priest Boukman, his leaders (among them Toussaint), and the blacks they incited swept from one village to another, torching buildings and killing every white man, woman, and child they saw. (Yes, it is true that the insurrectionists hoisted on high dead white babies impaled on their swords, but as to the report of cannibalism, which you inquired about, I have yet to receive confirmation.) The smell of that white massacre lingers on the air. I have been informed that for weeks the sky glowed with sheets of fire, and that more than 6,000 coffee plantations and 200 sugar refineries were destroyed. It is a chilling sound, these drums. Three are employed: the natives call them the Mama Drum, Papa Drum, and Baby Drum, and as they are played, the blacks perform a wild dance called the *Méringue*. I have personally witnessed them crooning a half-spoken, half-sung chant at their voodoo rites, where witch doctors transmogrify the dead—and sometimes living men—into zombies (The Enlightenment, I assure you, has yet to reach the outlying villages here), which are mindless slaves who do the bidding of their masters. (I've been told the witch doctors who conspired with Boukman and Toussaint took a special pleasure in turning their former owners into such spectral creatures.) For a white man, there is the fear here of being murdered in one's sleep. Since hearing of these unholy practices, my poor Cornelius has not slept well in days, and he screams at every sound in the night. I must assure him each evening that I keep a firearm by my bed in the room next to his own where my wife, Emma, and I sleep, and that we have trustworthy sentries—the more-Europeanized mulattoes—stationed with rifles just outside our doors.

Lately, I have been rereading your splendid *Notes on the State of Virginia,* partly because some nights sleep and I are strangers, and partly because my position as consul in the first all-black nation in the Western Hemisphere has whetted my curiosity to better understand what transpires beneath the ulotrichous skull of the Negro. You are right, I believe, when in your *Notes* you observe the inferiority of pure-bred blacks at Monticello, their childlike nature, their physical proximity to the apes, and their inability to grasp the arts and sciences as, for example, you have so wondrously done in your writings and studies on architecture, geology, natural history, and scientific farming. Clearly, as you state, the white race is blessed with greater beauty and in America is destined—as if by divine decree—to be the black man's master, to guide him as the parent does the child, and surely this is for the Negro's own good, lest he, in our state of freedom, fall deeper into savagery. No, none of these matters do I question as I revisit your *Notes*. But I have begun to wonder since our arrival at Le Cap, and after such close contact with Negroes like Jacques Dessalines (during their Revolution he cried to the other slaves, "Those who wish to die free, rally round me now," which is hardly different than our own Patrick Henry's "Give me Liberty or give me death"), if perhaps the lower standards and performance you so precisely observed in the Virginia slaves are not innate, after all, but rather the product of the severity of American slavery itself.

I venture this hypothesis, sir, only because in the blacks of St. Domingue, living now free of whites—Spaniards and Frenchmen—for the first time since 1512, I have seen a pride, independence, and ambition (as well as arrogance) that favors the confidence of our own patriots after they defeated King George. Nowhere is this pride more evident, or infectious, than in Le Cap, and in the person of the island's beloved leader, Toussaint L'Ouverture. As General Washington is to us, he is to them: a warrior legendary for his courage; the framer of their Constitution; and a statesman capable of forgiving his defeated enemies, for Toussaint has approved trade with France, and it is well known that he has sent both his sons to study at world-acclaimed institutions in Paris.

You will be interested to learn that after his cold rejection of my Commission, and of me as your consul, the governor-general relented and has now allowed me to visit with him on five occasions, the most recent being yesternight. Due to illness, my wife and son could not accompany me to dinner with Toussaint and other officials of this new republic. I must say I felt a bit light-headed during the aperitif, and a little off-balance in that dining room of stunningly beautiful mulatto ladies and darker-skinned heads of state, but I smiled until the muscles round my mouth began to ache, and drank as lustily as my hosts, who seemed—I was sure of this—amused by my discomfiture. Perhaps it was the wine, or my generally fatigued condition in this horseshoe-shaped country's merciless heat, but when I looked at the head of the table, where Toussaint sat, he presented a magnific figure of manhood, one far better-looking and more dashing in his French uniform and black knee-boots than that runt Bonaparte. Gradually, I began to see why his people called him L' Ouverture ("the Opener"), and then later added "Deliverer" to his many honorific titles. He chatted now with Jacques Dessalines, who sat at his right side, and with Henri Christophe, at his left, ignoring me deliberately for as much as fifteen minutes at a time, so that all I could do was stare down at my dinner plate, shoveling down the entrée, then dessert, in humiliating silence until he deigned to politely ask me a question about you, our system of government, or our relations with the French. I believe he deliberately seated me on a chair shorter than the others at the table, so that even the women looked down at me all during the meal. Try as I might, I could not intimidate him or the others with my superior breeding, credentials as a representative of the United States government, or the color of my skin, which before their Revolution would have been enough to make most slaves treat me with deference. No, none of that worked on them. All during that evening, after we'd eaten, I felt a sharp pain slice through my abdomen, but you will be relieved to know, sir, that despite my weakening condition I was alert and overheard Christophe discussing with Toussaint his idea for constructing a mountaintop fortress to protect this fledging nation from attack. He wants to call it the Citadelle. His plan is to equip it with 365 heavy bronze cannons.

I must confess, sadly, that as your consul it seems to me that Toussaint knows that, despite the decision of Congress to continue trade with St. Domingue, you—as our president—have no plans to support his Revolution, indeed, that you consider its leaders to be property that has illegally seized a freedom it does not deserve, and that their successful example of insurrection sends a dangerous message to Negroes on our shores. It is this suspicion of you that led to the poor treatment I received last night, and to Toussaint's remark to Christophe that his color alone was the reason you failed to send him a greeting.

These, as I say, are the tribulations I have endured in your service since my arrival, troubles I gladly endure for my country. I list them here only for one reason. As I was leaving the governor-general's mansion, almost doubled over by the recurrent complaint in my lower regions, but smiling nevertheless, shaking the hand of my host, then Christophe's, I came to Jacques Dessalines, and swung out my palm. He took it in a firm grasp, but then I *saw* it. Just for a moment. There, in his left hand, which he kept behind his back, Dessalines held a clay homunculus—a white doll—of *me*, one with a pin stuck in its belly.

Sir, I have barely started my tenure as consul in St.

Domingue. However, I pray you will consider the problems, political and personal, that my family and I have encountered and repeal my appointment. If you do not, I fear this may well be the last communication from

> *Your most obedient, and most obliged,*
> *And most dutiful humble Servant,*
> Theobald Wedgwood

The People Speak

A NEWS ITEM from the *Philadelphia Liberator*
(Philadelphia, Pennsylvania, January 16, 1817)

A Vote on Colonization

Yesterday a reported three thousand black people packed into Bethel Church to vote on a proposal by the newly created American Colonization Society that free blacks in the United States should be resettled in Africa. The tempestuous meeting, which lasted most of the day, and was peppered throughout by passionate speeches for and against the proposal, ended with a historic vote that will no doubt be decisive—if not fateful—for the future of all people of African descent in this nation.

Fiction often changes the facts for dramatic effect. Paul Cuffe did not attend the meeting described here, and he learned of the vote by letter. There were no women present, and the actual vote was by voice, not paper ballot. The author hopes readers of this tale can forgive the liberties taken with facts in order to conjure a moment in time with feeling.

It was, some observers remarked, a debate on two equally powerful yet antithetical dreams within the black American soul.

The meeting came but fifteen days after the founding of the American Colonization Society, a creation of Robert Finley that has been endorsed with enthusiasm by President James Madison and former president Jefferson. Its mission, according to its founder, is to redress the evils of exploitation visited upon Negroes in Africa, and to establish on that continent a homeland for American people of color, a place to which they can emigrate, live free from white persecution, and pursue their interests without interference. The idea has great popularity these days, among both blacks and whites, who question whether the Negro, once released from bondage, will ever be accepted in or assimilated by American society.

In attendance at Wednesday's gathering were some of the most prominent leaders and luminaries from Philadelphia's growing black community. On hand was the ubiquitous Rev. Absalom Jones; maritime entrepreneur Paul Cuffe and his Indian wife, Alice; businessman James Forten; and Rev. Richard Allen, who, as on many occasions previously, provided his church as the site for this great Negro debate and introduced Mr. Forten as the day's first speaker.

Taking the stage, Mr. Forten, fifty-one, explained how he was contacted by a representative of the American Colonization Society who sought his support in swaying Philadelphia's Negroes to the idea of leaving America. "You all know me and what I stand for," said Mr. Forten, his voice breaking with emotion. He reminded the gathering of his humble beginnings as a powder boy in the American Navy when he was fifteen, how at twenty he was foreman in a sail loft, and by age forty owned it and now employed more than forty men. "My life has been nurtured in the ground of this fledging nation," he said. "I have been an American *patriot* through and through, but I have also been one of this country's greatest critics as well."

He cited his "A Series of Letters by a Man of Color," composed four years ago, which opposed the legislature's attempt to force all blacks in the city to register, and his life-long work as an abolitionist. Mr. Forten then reminded the audience of how central Negroes have been to every dimension of life in the colonies, and how Crispus Attucks was the first to die opposing British tyranny.

"But despite our contributions to this country," Mr. Forten said, "we have not been—and perhaps will never be—accepted by its white citizens. And so, although it makes my heart heavy to do so, I intend to vote—as I hope you will—for taking my chances in the land of our forebears."

The audience was greatly moved by Mr. Forten's address. The applause lasted for several minutes.

He was followed by Paul Cuffe, fifty-eight, a Quaker who for over a decade, and long before the formation of the American Colonization Society, has urged free blacks toward expatriation. As reported earlier in this newspaper (September 8, 1815), Mr. Cuffe, owner of the 268-ton *Alpha*, is a man whose wisdom is seasoned by his world travels. Among his many vessels are sloops, schooners, and two brigs. He has sailed to Sweden and, on his ship the *Traveller*, visited Sierra Leone in 1811. There, he set up the Friendly Society, an organization dedicated to helping American blacks migrate to Africa. In fact, three years later Mr. Cuffe transported thirty-eight colored men and women to Sierra Leone and paid for their $4,000 voyage himself. A philanthropist, he created a school for Negro children on his farm and acquired a teacher for them.

As he walked slowly to the stage, still weak from a recent illness, a cheer rose from the gathering. Mr. Cuffe, smiling gently, waited patiently at the podium for the audience to settle down.

"Thank you," he said. "We are all old friends here and have suffered much together over the years. We struggled together thirty-seven years ago to protest taxation of our people when we have no representation. I led that fight, you'll recall. And twenty years ago, my friend there, Absalom Jones, spearheaded our effort to repeal the Fugitive Slave Act. We have all shed our blood for freedom, and of our triumphs I think we should be proud. But as an *old* fighter, one who has seen many campaigns to achieve justice for the colored people of America, I sometimes wonder how much farther we can go. I won't lie to you. I never have, and I can't start now. My doctor tells me I'll be lucky if I see Thanksgiving this year. With so little time, I think I should tell you the truth, at least as I've been privileged to perceive it.

"Here, in America, we face an uphill struggle. Our victories can be taken away with a single stroke of the pen by men like former president Jefferson. He and others like him have always envisioned the United States as a white man's nation, irrespective of our deep and enduring contributions to its economy, its culture, and its precious Revolution. I've never avoided a good fight in my life. You know that. But now, after much reflection, I believe it is time to withdraw from white men. Our great energies, talents, and love would be better applied, I think, to the nurturing of a democracy on the continent of our origin. Visit Sierra Leone, if you dare. I have. And it gladdened my heart to see Negroes who possessed every freedom this republic withholds from us. I say, my friends, that it is doubtful the black man and the white can ever live in harmony. Can *he* ever relinquish his desire to be dominant? Can *you* ever forget the horrors of our history in this country at the hands of white men? No, methinks it is asking too much for both sides, theirs and ours, to live peacefully as one people. Does that sound defeatist? If so, you hear me wrong. In the impossibility of the Madisons and Jeffersons ever treating us like equals there lies the great opportunity for you and I, as freemen, to return to our mother country with skills and knowledge that will raise that continent, benighted by centuries of slavery and oppression, to its rightful place as a powerful black presence in the world. Leave America to the white man. A far greater and nobler civilization beckons, if we but have the courage to answer its call."

When Mr. Cuffe was done, the church was silent for a moment. Then, spontaneously, those in attendance responded with thunderous applause.

Other leaders of the colored community took the podium for the next few hours, all passionately arguing to their unlettered brethren the position of emigration. At various times the assembly became raucous, with members of the audience shouting their positions from the floor, so that Rev. Allen found it necessary to bang his gavel over and over, calling for order. "Please settle down," he said. "Everyone will have a chance to speak. Gentlemen, remember what we are deciding here. It has taken the American Colonial Society to bring this crisis to the surface. We are at, I daresay, a crossroads. Future generations will judge us by our sobriety. Our wisdom—or our lack of it! We are voting—be advised—not merely on the future position of the Philadelphia Negro vis-a-vis America, but on which direction *all* our people will take in the future. Now, if you'll look to the rear of the room, you'll see ushers are moving down the aisles, each carrying a basket filled with ballots. I ask you to take one. Take a prayerful moment to review the discussion you've heard, then vote knowing your decision carries as much weight for the direction of this nation as that of the white men who assembled at the Constitutional Convention."

Concluding his instructions, Rev. Allen went back to his seat to vote. Ten minutes later, the votes were collected. The ushers took them into the back of the church to tally "yeas" and "nays" for the Society's proposal. As they worked, Bethel's choir sang two beautiful hymns. Before they could begin a third, one of the ushers, a young man, brought a slip of paper to Rev. Allen, who again stepped up to the podium. Those gathered grew quiet. Rev. Allen cleared his throat.

"You, the people, have voted unanimously against the position of your leaders," he said. "You have rejected returning to Africa. Whatever our future is to be, you have decided that it will be *here*, on these shores. God help us all…"

Soulcatcher

IN THAT BOSTON MARKET on a Thursday in 1853, there were two men, one black, one white, who were as intimately bound, in a way, as brothers, or perhaps it was better to say they were caught in a macabre dance, one that stretched from rural South Carolina to Massachusetts over a period of three long months of hiding, disguises, last-minute escapes, name changes, and tracking leads that led nowhere until it brought them both here to the bustling open-air market perched near the waterfront on a summer afternoon.

They were weary, these two. Hunter and Hunted.

The Hunter paused just at the periphery of the market, breathing in the salt-laced air, looking at the numerous stands filled with freshly baked bread, a variety of vegetables, fish caught earlier that day, and handicrafts—wood carvings, colorful quilts, and hand-sewn leather garments—sold by black and white Bostonians alike. The Negroes, he noticed, including the one he was looking for, had set up their stands toward the rear of the market, separating themselves from the others. A gnarled, little merchant with a

Scottish brogue, and wearing a yeoman's cap and burnoose, suddenly pulled at the sleeve of the Hunter's jacket. He pointed with his other hand at boots on the table beside him. Irritated, the Hunter shook loose his arm from the merchant's grasp, then moved on a few paces through the crowded market, tilting down his hat brim a bit to hide his face, and positioned himself to one side of a hanging display of rugs. From there he could see the Negro he wanted but was not himself in plain view. He reached into a pocket sewn inside his ragged, gypsy cloak, felt around his pistol—a Colt .31— and his fingers closed on a folded piece of paper. The Hunter withdrew it. He opened it slowly, as he'd done nearly a hundred times in the last three months in dozens of towns in North Carolina, Virginia, Pennsylvania, and New York, in daylight and dark, when the trail he was following went cold and he sat before a campfire, wondering how long it would be before he would collect his bounty. The paper had been folded and creased so often a few of the words on it were feathery. In the upper right-hand corner he saw the long-dried stain of dark blood—his brother Jeremiah's—and below it this notice:

RUN away from <u>Charlotte</u> on *Sunday,* a Negro slave named FRANK, well known about the Country as a craftsman, has a scar on one of his Wrists, and has lost one or more of his fore Teeth; he is a very resourceful Fellow, skilled as a smithy and saddlemaker, loves Drink, and is very often in his Cups, but surly and dangerous when sober. Whither he has run to, I cannot say, but I will offer $200 to have him returned to me. He can read and write.

APRIL 2, 1853   JUBAL CATTON

From where he stood, the Hunter had a side view of a black craftsman seated before a table of wood carvings, talking to a nearby old Negress selling fish and a balding black man hawking produce. The Hunter was sure this was Frank. When last he'd seen him—just outside Norfolk—he was wearing Lowell pants and a jerkin. Today he was dressed better in a homespun suit. Under the table, he noticed, there was a flask, which the Negro occasionally lifted to his lips, then slid back out of sight. For a time, the Hunter was content simply to study him. He didn't want to rush. That's what Jeremiah always told him: *You move too quick, you'll startle the prey. When the moment's right to move, you'll know.* Now that he nearly had Frank trapped, the Hunter wished his brother could be there, at the market, for the catch. But Jeremiah was back in Charleston. Blind. When Frank bolted from Jubal Catton's farm, he'd stolen his master's Walker .44, and when they found him hiding in a barn, Frank fired at Jeremiah's face from five feet away, missing him—the nigger was a bad shot—but the blast seared his brother's eyes. Yes, thought the Hunter. He wished like hell Jeremiah was here now. They both still wanted that reward. But this runaway had made the hunt personal. During the first month he pursued Frank, his intent was to kill him. Then, as the weeks drew on, he realized slavery was worse than death. It was a little bit of death every day. It was even worse than being blind.

He would take him back, the Hunter decided. Jeremiah'd want it that way.

The Hunted reached under his table, grabbed the bottle by its neck, then drank just enough to take away the dryness in his throat. He never knew exactly why, but for some reason he'd always fought better drunk than sober. And it looked like he had a fight coming now, though he had thrown away his master's gun and had nothing to defend himself with but his bare hands. He thought, *All right, if that's the way it has to be.* He'd seen the white man—his name was Clement Walker—the moment he entered the market, or rather his nerves had responded, as they always did, when a soulcatcher was close by. He could smell them the way a rabbit did a hound. It was the way they looked at colored people, he supposed. Most whites didn't bother to look at you at all, like you were invisible. Or as unimportant as a fence post. Or if they were afraid of you, they'd look away altogether. But not soulcatchers. They wanted to see your face. Match it with a description on a wanted poster. Oh yes, *they* looked. Real hard.

That was how he'd spotted the Hunter. But he didn't need that sixth sense anymore to recognize Walker. The Hunted rubbed his left shoulder, massaging the spot where the Hunter had months ago left a deep imprint of his incisors—this, during their tussle after he shot at Jeremiah Walker. No question he'd know Clement *anywhere.* The man was in his dreams or—more precisely—his nightmares since he left his master's farm. Not a day passed when Frank didn't look over his shoulder, expecting him to be there, holding a gun in one hand and manacles in the other. It was almost as if he was *inside* Frank now, the embodiment of all his fears.

His first instinct had been to flee when he saw him, but Lord, he felt tired of running. Of being alone. That he'd not counted on when he ran for freedom: the staggering loneliness. The suspicions. The constant living in fear that he might be taken back to the tortures of slavery at any time. For months, he'd been afraid to speak to anyone. Every white man was a potential enemy. No Negro could be fully trusted either. But along the way he'd been fortunate. More so than many fugitives. He met white ministers who were conductors for the Underground Railroad, men who fronted as his master long enough for him to traverse the states of North Carolina and Virginia; and here, in Boston, he'd found free blacks—the very portrait of Christian kindness and self-sacrifice—willing to risk their own lives to help him. They were deeply religious, these Negroes. Lambs of Jesus, he thought at first. They put him up in their homes, fed him, provided him with clothes and a fresh start. Even helped him pick a new name. Jackson Lee was the one he used now. And he deployed those many skills he'd learned as a slave, plus his own God-given talent, to rebuilding his life from scratch. At least, until now.

Out of the corner of his eye he could see the Hunter moving closer, circling round toward the front of the market, keeping the waterfront at Frank's back, to cut him off if he tried to run. This time the Hunted decided, no. He would stay, dying here among free black people. He'd been to their churches, heard their preachers say no man should fear death because the Son of God conquered that for all time. And no man could be enslaved, they said, if he was prepared to die.

The Hunter stopped in front of his table. He looked over the carvings, picked up one of a horse, and examined it, the faintest of smiles on his lips. "You do right fine work."

"Thank you."

"I once knew a fellah in Charleston was almost as good as you."

"That so?"

"Um-huh.' The Hunter put the carving down. 'Nigger named Frank. I don't suppose you know his work, do you?"

"No," he shook his head. "Never been to Charleston. Lived here my whole life. You kin ask anybody here 'bout that." He tilted his head toward the balding man, then at the old black woman selling fish. "Ain't that so?"

"Yes, sir." The balding man held out his hand at waist-level, his palm facing down. "I been knowin' Jackson since he was yea-high."

The old woman chimed in, "That's right. He belong to my church."

The Hunter's eyes narrowed, he looked at both of them irritably, said, "I think you two better mind your own damned business," then he swung his gaze back toward the Hunted. "I ain't here to play games with you, Frank."

"My name is Jackson Lee."

"Right, and I'm Andrew Jackson."

Slowly, the Hunter withdrew his pistol. His arm bent, close to his side, he pointed the barrel at the Hunted. "Get up."

Frank sat motionless, looking down the black, one-eyed barrel. "No."

"Then I'll shoot you, nigger. Right here."

"Guess you'll have to do that then."

The old woman said, "Mister! You don't have to *do* that!"

"Naw," the balding man pleaded. "He from round here!"

Frowning, the Hunter took a deep breath. "I *told* y'all to shut up and stay out of this! It ain't your affair!"

In the market there came first one shot, shattering the air. By the time the second exploded, merchants and patrons were screaming, scattering from the waterfront like windblown leaves, tipping over tables that sent potatoes, cabbages, and melons rolling into the street. When the thunderous pistol reports subsided, leaving only a silence, and the susurration of wind off the water, the only figures left in the debris of broken displays and stands were the Hunter—he was sprawled dead beneath a rug he'd pulled to the ground as he fell—and the Hunted. There were also his new friends: The black fish woman. The balding man. Both were members of Boston's chapter of the Liberty Association, devoted to killing bounty hunters on sight. The balding man was Frank's minister. The fish woman was the minister's mother. They were the ones who'd taken him in. Helped him set up his stall in the market. And they were much better shots than he was.

It was good, thought Frank, to have friends—hunters in their own right—like these.

A Lion at Pendleton

Am I sadly cast aside,
On misfortune's rugged tide?
Will the world my pains deride
Forever?

THE WHITE MOB in Pendleton, Indiana, had dragged him
from the outdoor platform in the woods, where he was de-
nouncing the evils of slavery, how it dehumanized Christian
masters and bondsmen alike—this, after the townspeople
had denied him use of the local Baptist church. His voice, a
bronze basso profundo, filled the woods, rolling over a
crowd that favored parishioners at a camp meeting. Delicate
white women in the front seats fainted (as they often did
when he spoke), partly because they had never heard a
Negro whose oratorical skills outdistanced even those of a
Cicero, and partly because of how this remarkable mulatto
looked: tall, muscular from a life of field work, ship caulking,
and handling coal, he stood before them broad-shouldered,
with a striking mane of obsidian hair, appearing for all the

world like a lion who'd decided one day to assume the shape of a man. This was the Frederick Douglass they'd read and heard so much about, of whom James Russell Lowell said, "The very look of Douglass was an irresistible logic against the oppression of his race." Oh yes, they fainted dead, these polite, white ladies in Pendleton, because he was Shakespearean in his bearing, more handsome than their husbands, with a voice that ran rill-like in their heads, and who could doubt the desire they felt for him, the fugitive slave who was the best thing that ever happened to the abolitionist movement, overshadowing even William Lloyd Garrison? To be honest, it was better to faint than face the troubling fact that they felt themselves melting in their seats when he turned his penetrating gaze their way.

No doubt the gang of white men who entered the woods noticed how Douglass ensorcelled their women, and for a moment they were mesmerized themselves, staring up in a few unguarded seconds of awe at the lion-become-man, who not only challenged every idea they'd ever believed about Negroes, but called in question their manhood as well. Could *they* have survived all he had? Wrestling with his master Thomas Auld's dogs (that were better fed than he was) over bones to feed himself? A whipping every week for six straight months from Mr. Covey, a well-known "negro-breaker" Auld had hired him out to when he was sixteen, and whom, once Douglass had had enough of this treatment, he had fought for two hours straight until the older man gave up, never raising a hand to him again or mentioning this shameful defeat to other white men? Could they have conceived his masterful plans for escaping bondage? Taught themselves (and other slaves) to read? No, they were not—and would never be—*his* equal. And so they fell upon him, there in the woods, tearing down the platform after hauling him from it (that took twelve grown men), with him trading two blows for each of theirs, shifting instantly from eloquent oratory to raining punches upon them that broke cartilage and bone until by the sheer weight of their numbers they pinned him down, kicked and pummeled him round his great head, and then at last left when he lost consciousness. They were bruised, bleeding from their noses, and limping, but they were sure the abolitionist nigger from New England was dead.

> *Must I dwell in Slavery's night,*
> *And all pleasure take its flight,*
> *Far beyond my feeble sight,*
> *Forever?*

He awoke, his head pounding, in the spare bedroom of Neal Hardy, one of his Quaker friends in Pendleton. Experimentally, he tried to sit up, felt a pain—prismatic in its complexity—pierce through his chest, and fell back with a moan onto his pillow, closing his eyes. Was he still alive? He wasn't sure at first. Did he still have all his teeth? Was it night or day? One of his hands, bandaged, was badly throbbing. Although it hurt to raise his arm, he did so, then poked the index finger of his unbandaged hand into his mouth, probing until he was satisfied that, yes, all his teeth were there. He took deep, long breaths just to see if he still could. If he didn't know better, he'd swear from the throbbing ache in his legs and arms that he was back on his pallet in the slave quarters of Edward Covey, who worked his bondsmen in all weather—indeed, worked beside them sometimes so he knew how much effort a chore demanded and if a slave was slacking off—and drove his field hands until they dropped. Or, if they endured his hellish regimen, they turned to drink to dull their minds when their master was not working them or watching them in secret.

Gradually, he opened his eyes again, peering from left to right, taking in a candlestand, a fireplace directly in front of him, and away to his right Neal Hardy, who sat in a ladder-backed chair, his long face full of sorrow.

> *Worst of all, must hope grow dim,*
> *And withhold her cheering beam?*
> *Rather let me sleep and dream*
> *Forever!*

"Fred," said Hardy, "you've been out a long time. We've been worried."

"Have I? What day is this?"

"Wednesday. It's almost midnight. We brought you to my home straightaway after those hooligans beat you this afternoon."

"Beat me? I barely remember it. I recall a fight, but I thought I was winning. Did I give as good as I got?"

Hardy smiled. "Better, given the odds. But for a little

while there I was afraid we were going to lose you. We *would* have lost any other man, but thank God you've got the constitution of a horse."

"A tired horse, I daresay." He struggled to sit up. Hardy quickly moved to his side, helping him as he winced, biting down on his lower lip, his eyes squeezed shut from the pain of changing his posture. "Thank you, Neal. I guess I'd better rest for a few hours before we move on to the next engagement tomorrow. Where is it?"

"Noblesville, but you're not going. I won't allow it."

"What's this now?"

"You heard me. That hand of yours is *broken*. And I'm not a doctor, so I pray my wife and I set it correctly. Not only do I want you in bed for the rest of the week, I'd like to have a doctor drop by in the morning to examine you for anything I might have missed. For all I know, the blows you took could prove fatal. Here now, look at me. How many fingers am I holding up?"

Actually, he wasn't sure. He squinted, seeing two, but...there was a hazy, wavering digit between them that might have been a third.

"I can *count*, Neal," he said, trying to dodge the examination. "And I *must* be in Noblesville tomorrow evening. I've been beaten before—you know that—at the hands of drunken slaveholders and other mobs drunk with hatred. They've not stopped me yet."

"No, they haven't. But *I* am. For a week at least." Hardy felt the orator's brow with his fingers, frowned at its warmth, then stepped toward the bedroom door. "We are not finished with Frederick Douglass. We need him too dearly to allow him to push himself into an early grave. I'll be just outside this door. Try to rest. *I* plan to. I'm too exhausted to even un-hitch the horses until morning—"

"Am I a prisoner then?"

"A guest! You've been on the road speaking for over a month now, traveling to five towns a week! That beating you took may be a good thing. It may be a blessing, God's way of telling you to slow down, for heaven's sake, in order to preserve yourself until this fight is over!" He paused, his voice and eyes softening. "Please do as I say. If anything happens to you, our cause will be severly impaired."

"As you wish. I'll rest."

"Good…and good night."

> *Something still my heart surveys,*
> *Groping through this dreary maze;*
> *It is Hope?—then burn and blaze*
> *Forever!*

He lay awake for hours, his body burning with injuries so varied, ranging from mild aches and tender spots to out-right agony in his broken hand, that he spent close to an hour marveling at just how badly white men had hurt him this time. Perhaps Neal Hardy was right. Since his escape to New Bedford in 1838 when he was twenty years old, since changing his name from Frederick Augustus Bailey to Fred-erick Johnson and at last to Frederick Douglass (an abolitionist friend, Nathan Johnson, suggested "Douglass" after reading *Lady of the Lake*, and he settled into that new incarnation), since the day the Massachusetts Anti-Slavery Society discovered his gifts and engaged him as a lecturer, he had not rested. Nor had he wanted to. How could his spirit sleep as long as a single black man or woman was in chains? But was he too wounded this time? Yes, he ached from chin to calves, but despite Hardy's obvious compassion and concern for his health, it annoyed him a little whenever white men told him what to do. He'd had quite enough of their hostile—or benign—advice when he was in bondage. If they could not truly understand all he'd endured or had not walked a mile in his boots (when he had boots, which was seldom during his childhood), then how could they recommend anything to him? And besides, most of the time their advice was wrong. Like the Massachusetts Anti-Slavery Society, which initially asked him only to describe his victimization as a slave, not launch into a devastating critique of the country as a whole—*that*, they told him, was the province of white men like the society's William Collins or the venerated Garrison. *Stay in your place* is what they were telling him, *We know best*. Well, they had not. Only he knew what was best for Douglass. They warned him against publishing an undisguised narrative on his life, insisting that such a document would reveal that he was Frederick Bailey, a runaway slave, and bring the slave catchers to his door. He'd thought, *Damn the slave catchers*, and planned one day to release his account of his life anyway, and if it brought him even greater fame than white freedom fighters or black ones, would that cause tension within the movement? If so, very well. He had no time for the petty reactions of lesser men, black or white.

> *Leave me not a wretch confined,*
> *Altogether lame and blind—*
> *Unto gross despair consigned,*
> *Forever!*

Yet perhaps—just perhaps—he should stay abed long enough to heal a little. If he needed convalescence it would give him time to write. His thoughts began to drift to possible subjects and alighted on the class of forty slaves he once taught to read on Sundays at the home of a free colored man. He was breaking the law, doing that. How might he describe them when time permitted him to turn to the narrative he hoped to compose?...

They were noble souls; they not only possessed loving hearts, but brave ones. We were linked and interlinked with each other...I believe we would have died for each other. We never undertook to do anything, of any importance, without a mutual consultation...We were one...When I think that these precious souls are to-day shut up in the prison-house of slavery, my feelings overcome me, and I am almost ready to ask, "Does a righteous God govern the universe? and for what does he hold the thunders in his right hand, if not to smite the oppressor, and deliver the spoiled out of the hand of the spoiler?"

He sat bolt upright in bed, the sudden move sending pain through his back. But, no! He must not rest. They were still in bondage, those others, suffering like the slave in George Moses Horton's tragic poem. Waiting for him...

> *Heaven! in whom can I confide?*
> *Canst thou not for all provide?*
> *Condescend to be my guide*
> *Forever!*

With an effort that brought beads of glistening sweat to his forehead, he climbed down from the bed, swinging his feet over the side first, then standing. The room spun. He steadied himself by gripping the ladder-backed chair with his good hand. (*Would the injured one,* he wondered, *ever heal?*) His clothes were on the chair. Slowly, he pulled them on with one hand. Given his injuries, dressing took an hour. When he was fully clothed, he padded quietly to the bedroom door, opened it cautiously, and found Hardy just outside the room, where he'd promised to be, but sleeping, his arms crossed over his chest and head tilted forward.

He tipped past him, exited through the house's rear door, and made his way to Hardy's carriage. The horses were still hitched to it, hardly a situation his host would have allowed under normal circumstances, but Lord knew they'd had an extraordinary day in Pendleton. He pulled himself up onto the seat. He took the reins in his left hand, snapped them, and geed the horses out onto the dark road. If he drove through the night and morning surely he would be in Noblesville in time for his next speech: yet another nail driven into slavery's casket. And if his death delivered his loved ones to freedom *one* day sooner, then so be it. Hardy, he supposed, would be upset when he awakened, discovering him and his horses gone. But this Quaker friend would know where to find him. Possibly he would follow him to Noblesville, arriving just toward the end of his engagement—a little late, as white men fighting oppression often were. And perhaps he would understand why his guest left. If Hardy did not, more's the pity, for, as he drove the horses on through the darkness, he did not have a spare moment to explain. Or to wait for white men—even the good ones—to catch up to him.

> And when this transient life shall end,
> Oh, may some kind, eternal friend,
> Bid me from servitude ascend,
> Forever!

The Mayor's Tale

ONCE UPON A TIME in a nation not very old the people of a large, northeastern city awoke one morning and discovered to their surprise (though they should have seen it coming) that something had changed in their lives.

The city's Mayor like many others went to sleep the night before, curled beneath the warm covers beside his Wife, feeling as he drifted off to sleep that all was well in the world. Their two children rested comfortably down the hallway in the great, three-story house; they were doing well at their studies, according to the tutor he'd hired for them, and it was likely both boys—then ages eight and twelve—would easily be accepted at the nation's oldest and most prestigious college when the time came for them to apply. His investments were performing better than expected, given the country's delicate political situation (but when, after all, was politics not a delicate matter?). Added to which, he'd worked hard all throughout 1850 to beat his competitors in neighboring cities along the eastern seaboard for a few lucrative contracts that would further industrialize his own city, which would assure his reelection, and he was meeting with representatives of those companies in the morning. Furthermore, his Wife of twenty years seemed pleased with her personal affairs, the charity work she and her friends did each weekend, and particularly with her abolitionist activities. He, being a progressive man, supported fully this cause of Negro manumission, both in his role as Mayor and, even more importantly, in his home, where he employed five free Negroes as servants. Indeed, he had cheered on and publicly supported the recent Compromise that abolished the slave trade in the District of Columbia. He treated his black help royally, or so the Mayor believed, and he overlooked what everyone in his social circle agreed were inherent and unfortunate deficiencies in colored people. These shortcomings, after all, were not *their* fault, but rather the unjust distribution of talent, beauty, and intelligence by Nature, so that those more generously endowed by Providence were duty bound to help them. Without white men, the Negro would be lost. They were like children in their dependency. The Mayor paid his servants handsomely and on time, was lavish with tips, inquired frequently into their health and well-being, told them repeatedly they were an important part of his family, and he proudly pointed them out when his friends, business associates, and political colleagues dined with his family or dropped by. And, as if that were not enough, the Mayor had a lovely, new mistress—a young singer of thirty (which was half his age), who gave him good reason to look forward to those weekends his Wife and her friends were away.

Yes, all was well—as well as a civilized man might expect—in the world on Wednesday, January 1, 1851.

Thursday, however, was quite another story. When he opened his eyes and stretched, having slept well—the sleep of the just, he'd say—the Mayor felt as rested as he did on Saturday, the day he normally slept in. But this wasn't the weekend. Or was it? For a moment he wasn't sure. He shook his Wife's shoulder, rousing her awake, and she said, "Why are you still here? Aren't you supposed to be at City Hall?" Like Immanuel Kant, the Mayor preferred his life "to be like the most regular of regular verbs." So he was at first bewildered, then upset, by this disruption of his schedule. He stumbled from bed, his bare feet landing on a floor so cold its chill went through him like a shock, squeezed a whoop from his lips, and sent him hopping around the room for his slippers. He found his wire-rim spectacles on a nightstand, then shivering so badly his teeth chattered, he bent over to better see the small, wooden clock. It was quarter past eleven. He'd slept all morning, missing at least five appointments.

And all the fireplaces were dark and cold.

The Mayor rang for his butler, Henry, who always awoke him and had each fireplace blazing by 5 A.M. No answer. He rang again, waiting and watching his breath steam the bedroom air as if he were standing outside on the ice-cold street. "Please get him to light the fireplaces *now!*" wailed his Wife. "I'm not leaving this bed until the house is warm! And tell the maid I'm *hungry!*" The Mayor sighed and said, "Yes, dear, I...I will. Henry must be sick this morning—he's never been remiss in his duties before, you know." He hurried to dress himself, and found to his great dismay that not only had his personal servant failed to wake him, but Henry had not prepared or set out his clothing for the day either. Because he was so late and had no idea where Henry put his freshly pressed linen, the Mayor grumbled and pulled on his wrinkled shirt from the day before (on the front was a red soup stain from a lunch he'd taken at his club, but he couldn't worry about that now), his uncreased trousers, his coat, then hurried downstairs and through the frigid hallways of his many-roomed house, calling for their servants. Again, there was no answer. In the kitchen, in the chambers set aside for their live-in help, and in the livery stable there was only silence. And not a black face to be found. Moreover, the horses had not been groomed. Or fed. His carriage was not ready. He would have to travel, he realized, the five miles to City Hall under his own locomotion!

Not being accustomed to walking, it took the Mayor two hours to traverse the distance between his home and office. He stopped to rest often, puffing, placing his hand against a wall, his heart racing and empty stomach growling. And what he saw—or rather didn't see—along the way to work startled him. There were no black people. It wasn't as if he looked for them every day. No, most of the time they blended into the background of his city, as unnoticeable as trees or weather vanes or lampposts—or maybe like the inner workings of a finely tuned watch. Obviously, no one paid attention to a timepiece's hidden mechanism until it ceased to work. But now, along the five-mile stretch between his home and City Hall, he saw chaos. Coal had not been delivered to homes, and this was the dead of winter! Barges had not been unloaded in the harbor. Fresh bread had not been delivered from bakeries. Roadwork lay unfinished, as if the fingers of God had plucked its dusky crews off the face of the earth. No windows were washed. No snow was shoveled. It was as if his city had run out of its primary source of power, coal. (A terrible pun, he knew, but on this awful day it seemed appropriate.) He wondered aloud as he galumphed down the nearly empty streets, "What in heaven's name is going on?" No carriages, driven by black coachmen, bore white passengers to and from the offices where they conducted the country's crucial business, domestic and international. Indeed, half the offices he saw were closed.

It was, therefore, a befuddled and disheveled Mayor who finally reached City Hall by 2 P.M. and slumped heavily behind his desk, wondering if his heart might fail him once and for all after his morning's exertions. Everything he'd accomplished this morning (which wasn't much) had taken two—perhaps three—times longer to do. His secretary, a young man named Daniel, looked very sad that Thursday. He told the Mayor the people with whom he'd missed appointments were furious. Two entrepreneurs of enormous wealth and influence who'd traveled a great distance to see him—one a railroad man, the other a maritime merchant—felt insulted by what they called Hizzoner's "malfeasance" and planned to cancel further discussions of their proposed contracts and in the future only do business with other cities.

"No!" whispered the Mayor.

His secretary said, "I'm afraid so, sir. Your political rivals will make great capital of this. Your reelection is only months away, and you promised in the last campaign to improve commerce, shipping, and transportation."

"I *know* what I promised, damn it!" The Mayor pounded his desk. "But it's not my fault! Nothing's been normal today!" He leaned back in his seat, red-faced, and began pulling at his fingers. "All the Negroes are gone. Have you noticed that? What on earth happened to them?"

"What *you* agreed to, I guess," said his secretary.

"*Me?* What are you babbling about, man? Talk sense! I never told the Negroes to go away! Have you been drinking?"

"No, sir. I'm quite sober, insofar as it appears we both will be out of a job by November. I'm referring to the Compromise in Congress, which you fully endorsed."

"What does *that* have to do with our Negroes being gone?"

Quietly, his secretary stepped from the Mayor's office to his own room, then returned after less than a minute with a copy of a newspaper from the day before. "Perhaps you should read this. Please read it *carefully*, sir. Meanwhile, if you don't mind, I'd like to repair to my office in order to finish sending out copies of my rèsumè to potential, future employers. And I have a dreadful headache today..."

His secretary departed, leaving the Mayor more baffled

than before. He opened the day-old newspaper, and there it was, the complex Compromise. In it, California became the thirty-first state. New Mexico and Utah were to be organized as territories and residents could decide for themselves whether to be free or slave. The slave trade was ended in D.C., and—*Wait!* He looked nearer, bringing the paper closer to his eyes in order to read some changes in the Fugitive Slave Act of 1793. Vaguely, he recalled this item, but hadn't attended closely to its details. Under the amendment, federal commissioners were granted the power to issue warrants for runaway slaves. They could form posses to capture fugitive blacks. They could fine citizens if they refused to help in returning Negroes to their former masters, who had to do nothing more than submit an affidavit in court. The blacks were denied a jury trial. They could not testify to defend themselves. Slowly, he put the newspaper down. His man Henry…their cook…their three other servants and perhaps *all* the coloreds in his city were runaways. No doubt they'd changed their names. And once they learned of the amendment to the Fugitive Slave Act, they'd fled en masse during the night, probably to Canada. Who could blame them? And *he* had endorsed this disaster?

Gloomily, the Mayor left City Hall. Night was coming on…and streetlamps were unlit. He plodded on, realizing that until now he'd not seen how dependent the life of the city—and his own fortune—was on blacks. They were interwoven, albeit invisibly, into the fabric of everything; and, like the dangling string on a sweater which, if pulled, unraveled the entire garment, so too their removal caused everything—high and low, private and personal—to collapse. Without sealing the deal on those contracts, he would lose his office. He was certain of that now. His own businesses would suffer. My God, he might even lose his mistress and be left with only his Wife, who sometimes could be a shrew! Miserably, he tramped back home in the snow, which seeped into his shoes and dampened his feet so thoroughly he felt his toes had frozen in one solid block of flesh by the time he reached his front door, coughing, his nose burning and running badly, because—yes—he'd picked up a nasty cold.

The house was colder and darker than before. If anything, he only wanted a little sympathy now from his Wife. He did not see her downstairs. So, blowing his nose into his handkerchief, he climbed the steep stairs to their bedroom, dripping all the way. "Dear," he said, opening the door, "I have some bad news..."

"Well," she crabbed, "you can save whatever it is until you find dinner for us. I haven't eaten all day. I'm *starving!* And so are the children!"

It dawned on him that she had not left their bed all day. "You couldn't find something for yourself in the kitchen?"

"Nothing's prepared! I haven't had to cook in years! You know that. I want you to go out right now and find us something to eat."

"Now?"

"Yes, *now.*"

Slump-shouldered, feeling euchered, the Mayor went back outside, walking two miles in the darkness, with fresh snow beginning to fall, flaking on his shoulders. An hour later he arrived at the building that housed his club, thinking perhaps there they would wrap four plates of food, which he could carry home to his family. He tried the door. It was locked. Inside no lights were on whatsoever. Then he saw a sign in the ground-floor window. NO WAITERS OR COOKS TODAY. He stared blankly, helplessly, at the words. His mouth wobbled. *Of course*, he thought, *Of course*...

And then Hizzoner broke down and wept in the snow.

Murderous Thoughts

"ALL RIGHT, YOU CAN interview me if you wish, but there's really not much to say. I think that white bier you see swinging over the street, just above our heads, with the legend THE FUNERAL OF LIBERTY says it all. Or over there—do you see it?—the union flag hanging upside down? Or there, on those shopkeepers' windows? They're draped in black because today we have collectively committed suicide in Boston. That's why you've got twenty thousand people out here today. We are dead. We are mourning *ourselves* as much as we are the decision that went against Anthony Burns. By returning that colored man to his master we have thoroughly undone the Revolution. We are not who we say we are. There's nothing left, I'm telling you, but lies and hypocrisy. And so I feel ashamed to wear this uniform. What's that? Yes, I resigned this morning as captain of the watch. Until this trial—this mockery of justice—came along, I was damned proud to be a Marine. My grandfather was with General Washington at Valley Forge. I grew up hearing stories every night at the dinner table about how the Tree of

Liberty is watered with the blood of patriots. That's Jefferson, in case you didn't know, and from the time I was a boy I have believed that sentiment, sir, with all my heart and soul. I cut my teeth on the words of Thomas Paine. On his belief that our Revolution, our freedom, was worth protecting with my life, if need be. I was a soldier. My daily bread was duty and obedience to the nation I served. So yes, I suppose it seems odd that I disobeyed a direct order from my commanding officer to escort Burns from his jail in the courthouse in order for *this* contingent of men to march him back into bondage. But it's *not* odd, I'm saying. You can quote me on that. My refusal to be a party to the enslavement of another human being is of a piece with my grandfather's resistance to British oppression during the war. There's the rub! D'you see what we've become? By holding the Negroes in slavery *we* are the very enemy we fought in 1776. As a patriot to the *principle*, if not this wretched Government that intensified the Fugitive Slave Act four years ago, I have chosen to leave the military that has been my life. Now tell me again, what newspaper did you say you represent?"

"Disappointed? Why yes, I suppose you can say that. I've been here in Boston for the last month on business. What is my business? Tobacco. My home is Charleston, and what that means is that I know a great deal more about Negroes and their needs than do you northerners. I've watched this trial, you know, for the last nine days. By *my* calculations, the cost of returning this runaway to his owner is a riot, the

life of one U.S. marshal, and $50,000, which must be taken
from the public treasury. No doubt the North will find a
new way to tax the South to pay for the expenses. From my
hotel window I saw the abolitionists when they stormed the
southwest door of the courthouse, determined to break out
this nigra Burns and set him free. I was watching too when
it was over and the body of that marshal's deputy was
brought outside. What *I* wish to know is why no one has
called that criminal action by its proper name: *treason*. It is
blatantly against recent legislation, and the Constitution, to
harbor or abet a fugitive nigra. He is property, first and fore-
most. If you were in that courthouse on the last day of the
trial, as I was, you would have seen the recognition in
Burns's eyes when his master appeared—it was the look of a
craven, guilty animal cornered at last. But was *any*one here,
in this city, at all pleased that the rightful goods of an honest man were restored? That today the law is being en-
forced? Hardly. And *that* is why I am illy pleased. Nay,
disgusted. If this tenuous union is to prevail, which I doubt
increasingly every day I am in Boston, then you Yankees
must honor the customs and way of life in the southern
states. You must—I put it to you, sir—stop this rape of *our*
rights. Oh, you don't agree with me? Then consider these
facts: since declaring independence, the United States has
acquired 2,373,046 square miles of territory from which it
has excluded the South. But it is the slavery question that
stings us most. On this the North has been irrational.
You—and your agitators for Negro manumission who now
control the Government—force the South to choose between

abolition or secession. We have no *say* in this Government. None a'tall! As John C. Calhoun put it, what was once a constitutional federal republic has been subverted and transformed into one that is as absolutist as that of the Autocrat of Russia. Can you see the South's position? *My* position? I do not want my businesses destroyed. My liberties rescinded. Or to see an inferior race released upon the South to wreak havoc with all that is genteel, civilized, and sanctioned by the Almighty. But that is what is happening day after day, and it will result—mark my words—in the dissolution of the union. No, if you knew the Negro better, you would not have such a long face today. But enough! This insufferable Government will be the ruin of us all..."

"Aye, guv'nor, I think it's a pitiful sight! All those soldiers and a cannon just to send one poor black devil back into slavery? Sweet, merciful Heaven, what's to become of us! What'd ye say? That's right I owns this bakery behind us. Worked on ships twelve years afore I could buy it. And it was me put black drapery in the window this morning. Sure now, I worked beside coloreds, unloadin' boats when they come in, and far as I can see they're no diff'rent than other blokes here in Boston. I'd wager a few are *better* citizens. They have to be. Some of 'em are fugitives, sure enough. They run here to get away from their bloody owners, find wives and husbands, and start families. And what's this new law say? I'll tell ye! It says a man kin be torn away from his rightful wife and wee li'l ones, put in chains like that fellah

Burns, and taken back to a life of torture. Anyone kin see why this city is under martial law. No self-respectin' Christian can just stand by and watch the Devil at work right outside his door. No, guv'nor, if we don't right this wrong—and bloody soon—we all deserve to burn in hell."

"You want to know about *that* night? Fine, then, I'll tell you, but only if your newspaper prints *exactly* what I say. And as I say it. After Anthony was captured and locked away in the courthouse, a public meeting to discuss his plight was called at Faneuil Hall. The time was seven o'clock. *I* should have been on my way to work at the hotel. I'm a waiter, and a damned good one, but I saw the notice of what they were doing to this black man. I couldn't carry on as if everything was normal, now could I? So I went to the meeting at Faneuil Hall. I sat for an *hour* listening to the city's important colored and white men debating the question of what to *do* about poor Anthony's imprisonment. You know, it's always this way when whites and Boston's officially chosen black spokesmen are brought together to confront the evils of oppression. Nothing happens but *talk*. Guilty whites bare their souls. They listen, oh so sympathetically, to handpicked representatives of the Negro community narrate a litany of abuses they've endured since childhood. And nothing gets done! I *hate* those meetings. I've been to dozens of them, and after every one the whites feel *so* much better about themselves because they spent an evening with their darker brothers, and the official Negroes—oh, let me tell you!—they *use* those meetings to emotionally blackmail white people, wringing concessions out of them for their own personal advancement. I left in disgust with a friend of mine, another waiter, who informed me that only a few blocks away another gathering of only blacks was about to take place to decide what to do about Anthony. We went there straightaway. The room held about ten men and women. There wasn't a Negro spokesman anywhere to be seen. The talk was over in *ten* minutes, I tell you! For what was there, after all, to discuss? A man was being enslaved. We had to *free* him. Period. Fifteen minutes after my friend and I arrived, we were all out on the street, moving on the courthouse, battering at its door. When word of our attack reached Faneuil Hall—where they were *still* talking, trying to determine what to do—the hall emptied, and they joined us in our assault. As you know, we were beaten back by the guards, and driven away, but not before that marshal's deputy was killed. No, I cannot tell you how he died. But when he did, that was all the excuse the authorities needed for bringing in eight companies of militia and the United States Marines. The sight of them on the streets makes me sick. They are arrogant! Worse, they tell me that the Government is a willing accomplice in this crime against Anthony Burns. Would that I could *do* something! You know, blacks comprise almost the entire class of waiters here in Boston. We took a vow—all of us—to refuse to serve *any* of the soldiers who have taken over this city. It's a small thing, I know. But during this crisis even meager acts of resistance are better than none at all. And whose side, pray, are *you* on?"

"You want *my* opinion of this affair? Mine? Do you know who I am? For your information, I am a mystic, a Transcendentalist, and a natural philosopher. I have been imprisoned by this Government for refusing to pay my poll tax, the reason being that I knew it was applied to the support of slavery. I have spoken with John Brown. I am, you should know, an advocate of civil disobedience. And you still want to quote me? Very well. Write this down, young man: *My thoughts are murder to the State today.* Little by little, week by week, I have watched the American government lose its integrity. Now it endeavors to make all of us agents of injustice. One can no longer be associated with it except in disgrace. Look around you right now. D'you see that detachment of lancers marching in front of Anthony Burns? They are unthinking *machines* of the State, serving it with their bodies, and they command no more respect from me than men of straw or a lump of dirt. And over there, in the courthouse, we have legislators, politicians, and lawyers who serve the State with their heads, though they rarely make any moral distinctions, and thus are as likely to serve the Devil, without intending it, as God. All of them tools of the State, not men, and the slave Government that is their master has on this day forced them to commit a crime against humanity. My advice to all Anthony Burns's friends who call themselves abolitionists is that they should effectually withdraw their support, both in person and property, from the Government of first Massachusetts, then the United States. They must see that the only social obligation any of us have is to do at any time what we know is right. They must be willing to go to prison for their beliefs, just as Anthony Burns is now being led to a lifelong prison sentence; they must, I am saying, get it into their heads, once and for all, that any State that can do to a man what we have done today must be torn down, destroyed, and let the Devil take the hindmost. Then, when this stain on our souls has been scrubbed away through Revolution, perhaps men and women of God, blacks and whites, can rebuild America with wood less crooked than that used by the Founders. Did you get all that? Even the part about Government officials? Good. Now please excuse me. I must return to my room for a time to write down all the details I can remember of this monstrous day. One of the most important things we can do, young man, is never forget…"